# a grain of truth
# a pinch of salt

c v williams

First edition: Sydney 2016
Publisher: Sydney School of Arts & Humanities
15-17 Argyle Place Millers Point NSW 2000
www.ssoa.com.au
a grain of truth a pinch of salt
ISBN: 978-0-9954219-4-3 print book
ISBN: 978-0-9954219-5-0 ebook
Copyright ©C V Williams, 2016.

Cover design by Ferdinando Manzo. Text design by Ferdinando Manzo. Typeset in Times New Roman. Printed and bound by Lightning Source as a POD paperback.

National Library of Australia Cataloguing-in-Publication data:
C V Williams, author.
a grain of truth a pinch of salt /C V Williams.
Fiction – short story – literary fiction – Australian stories – Australian fiction

# Dedication

For all those people who have encouraged me in living and writing.

# Acknowledgements

I would like to thank many people whose names I may not even now know who have given me opportunities to practise or publish my fictional writing. Michael Wilding (Sydney University), Gillian Dooley (Flinders University) and Nicholas Birns (New York University) stand out among them, as do the editors of some other academic journals. News editors, including the late Bert Christie (ABC Radio Newsroom) and Jack Waterford (The Canberra Times), took my efforts seriously, even in the midst of daily news deadlines. I also thank my family for the puzzled patience they have shown in indulging my writing obsessions.

My thanks to Transnational Literature (Flinders University) for publishing 'Balmy Bali' (Vol. 3 no. 2, May 2011); 'Pearly Shells' (Vol. 4 no. 2, May 2012); 'Over Seas' (Vol. 3 no. 1, November 2010); 'A Footnote on Footlights' (Vol. 5 no. 2, May 2013); and 'A Green Thumb and a Lotus Hand' (Vol. 1 no. 2, May 2009) http://fhrc.flinders.edu.au/transnational/home.html

Thanks also to Central Queensland University for publication of 'Trust' (Confessions and Memoirs: National Anthology of New Australian Writing 2006 p. 217-218, first published in 'Best Stories Under the Sun' Vol. 3 2005) and 'Travelling with Ganesh' ('Travellers' Tales: Best Stories Under the Sun', Vol. 2 2005 p. 180-185).

My appreciation is here acknowledged for the first publication of 'Anticipation' in Antipodes (December Vol. 21 no. 2 2007 p. 150-153)

Finally, I want to acknowledge staunch friends, Catherine Bloor, Sharon Dean and Lisa Creffield for editing and advice, and Ferdinando Manzo for text design and formatting, including cover design. I'm also grateful to the Sydney School of Arts & Humanities writing groups which have provided an empathetic background for my work over recent years.

# Contents

## Whose nose was this?

A blessing, now a curse? How could Lord Ganesh abandon her so? If there's any god who rules over noses it would have to be Ganesh, she thought. He'd been significant to her ever since she'd felt his 'presence' not only on a trip to India, his icon peeping out from crevices and corners in hotel foyers, restaurants, forecourts, bus stations, train arrival and departure halls, but also once during love-making, within her very being. Both forms of manifestation she'd written about and published to either enlighten or entertain the world, whichever any reader might prefer.

That was then. This was now – and Cassie had a skin cancer on the left side of her nose and even inside, its tentacles grasping at her flesh and pulsing into her gristle. The cancerous condition, caused by excessive sunbaking in her youth, used to be called a rat, for its inevitable nibbling away at the nostrils and very core of the noses of sufferers. A rat? But isn't that Ganesh's mascot? She'd have to check that. Yes, Ganesh or Ganapati, rides on a rat to symbolise his ability to destroy every obstacle in much the same way rats are able to gnaw through most materials. In any case, if this Hindu god had been so protective and pliable to her mindset, perhaps he was so for everyone – even for those who prayed for ill towards others. She wondered …

Stricken physically and emotionally, all she could think to do at the beginning of the prognosis was to take down the image of a fulsome belly, thick curling trunk and long eyelashes from her Facebook page, replacing it with a photo of herself. Yes, that was appropriate after all as it was her page, not Ganesh's. Perhaps she hadn't shown him the respect he was due. Though she'd intended no harm. He'd meant more to her than mere decoration; she had experienced the good he proffered. So she couldn't imagine the All-powerful would give way to petty, evil spell-casting.

Yet the diagnosis coincided so exactly with some other horrendous news. Tend to the present and the future will bring you emotional and physical prosperity, she counselled herself.

Perhaps it was the niggling feeling of a curse on her that led Cassie, all unknowing, to a tiny jewellery shop she'd visited now and then over the years, to chat with the jeweller who had a special interest in traditional Indian silver and gems. They got to yarning, as usual, as he scoured the store for some piece or other that would inspire her quirky mind to make a purchase. One story led to another until, suddenly, she stood rigid and alert as he showed her a partly battered ancient silver pendant, with the words 'You see this one is not as smooth as the other, but it's the more valuable piece because it has the serpent. It's what all daughters-in-law want to own to protect them from the dreaded mother-in-law'.

Cassie stared at the pendant – and the curled snake, ready to strike, had a powerful effect on her imagination. Yes, of course the undamaged pendant looked superficially better, but the serpent was mesmerising, and who would be prepared to pass it over in favour of a weaker model with its image absent. Cassie could almost see the many dark-skinned hands that had clasped it over decades, perhaps even centuries, the breasts that had supported it, the hopes that had been implanted in every graze and cut in the metal. It had been cherished and in return had provided the needed service of guarding its owners from harm, or at least some succour.

Cassie cradled the piece gently, in earnest. Whatever cuts and bruises lay ahead, she would literally 'face' them with confidence taken from this uncanny reassuring keepsake. She paid whatever was due, took the little cloth purse containing so much 'spiritual power' and later looped the length of silver chain over her head to rest the pendant on her chest. It depicted Ram Dev, a folk hero, who would use the serpent's power in her and, hopefully, Ganesh's cause.

Ganesh's pot belly was usually encircled by a snake, Cassie remembered. It was the cobra associated with Shiva, as a reminder that Ganesh is the son of the God Shiva. A relationship in tune with that of Jesus Christ, the son of God, his ultimate power working through the ever so compassionate patron of animals, St Francis, after whom the hospital where Cassie would have her operation, was named.

She had told a few friends of her impending clash with a cutting instrument, and was surprised to find that one workmate, Anna – short for Angel – had had the very same operation about ten years before. There was hardly a mark on her cheek or nose, only a very fine white line running down from her nose to near the corner of her upper lip, and a tiny notch on the flare of her nose.

Cassie complimented Anna on the faintness of the scar, as she'd never noticed it before and then, laughing, told her she'd been disappointed that Ganesh hadn't protected her own nose more attentively. After all, he was the King of Noses, surely.

'Yes,' Anna agreed. 'And you'd think he would have looked out for me, because Ana* means elephant in some Indian language!'

'I thought an 'ana' used to be the smallest coin in the Indian currency,' Cassie giggled. 'Before the paisa was introduced – and worth much less than a rupee. Ha! Maybe that does make sense. Being so tiny it must have been given this giant's name as a joke!'

So she and Anna were on the same irrational wavelength. It cheered Cassie to have a 'comrade-in-arms' – or more accurately 'comrade-under-the-knife'. Oh well, jokes aside, she'd have to work at the fear factor now, the fear of leaving a cancer in her body, rather than the vanity aspect of her ordeal to come. She would call on Ganesh to have this obstacle to her health, the basal cancer, removed with as little damage to her looks as possible.

No novice to surgery, during her first appointment with the plastic surgeon Cassie scrutinised the hands of the fellow in whose hands she would be placed – large, capable, very white with some freckling, they reminded her of her mother's side of the family. Dr Seamus Ryan had an educated Australian accent but his surname dated from the 12th century, even before the Domesday Book of recorded family names, and before a diaspora of poverty-stricken English families migrated to Ireland, then the United States and far flung

Australia! Generations of kind hands had been lovingly patting and stroking their way down through the centuries to deposit this particular descendent of theirs into a Catholic hospital in Sydney where he'd been dispensing good advice, and cutting flesh as an essential service, for probably forty years. What he didn't know about fussing, fidgeting and fiddling with facial features wasn't worth knowing. He even gently chucked her under the chin as he dispensed his perpetually cheery manner. Thinking of her mother made Cassie cry … it was her mother who would have been the most upset of any of Cassie's loved ones to see her daughter's scarred face. But Cassie was comforted in knowing her mother was spared that sadness by her own death a few years before. She felt at least that consolation.

Think in a positive way about how the surgery will go, was Dr Ryan's take-home message, delivered with an invincible confidence.

Within weeks, the day of the operation arrived and as Cassie drove to the hospital, her mind couldn't resist the urge to imagine, over and over, the slice of a scalpel down her cheek, running along the length of her nose. The surgeon had already sketched the trail it would take. He'd even spoken about the possible need to cut a part of the top of her ear to insert in the flare of her left nostril. What? There was only one person she knew who'd had a part of his ear cut off from a visit to the barber when he was a boy! The surgeon also pointed out that one of his nostrils had no air passage ever since he'd been patched up after an injury in his youth, as a warning that the operation might also rid her of this capacity. He gave her copious description of the 3-part procedure to take out her offending cancerous lump, extracting the wayward basal cancer, digging out flesh above it to fill in the hole, and then pushing fat across from her cheek to fill the second hole. It sounded grotesque. How could she keep uppermost in her mind the dire consequences of ignoring this call to submit to the crafty patchworking of her fine flesh? The removal would cover a diameter of 14 mm. It had to be done now or the size of the lump would leave an even bigger hole, or worse, it would be too late to operate. The digging had to start.

The operation, planned as an hours' duration, lasting two and a half, was over and she was drifting in mind and spirit as she effusively gave thanks all round and was wheeled to a ward for an overnight stay. Painkillers and an ice pack were her bedfellows through the dark hours – along with nurses, a Declan and a Patrick, coming and going with soft steps and quiet words. Her mother hovered in the shadows …

The next day Cassie looked a horror when she peered with one eye at what used to be her identity. When the left eye patch was taken off, she took a selfie – and then stared at it with a mix of disgust and awe. Whose nose was this – enormous and covered by a thick bandage?

Staring back at her was just a slight variation of the picture of Ganesh she kept in her car as a reminder of her capacity to enjoy life. But here she wasn't enjoying life. Ganesh had taken over her face – similar eyes, similar trunk, similar wrinkles, plus an enormous increase in size as a result of swelling. Even the touches of red he loved to have about him were illustrated in blood. Ganesh was truly lord of new beginnings and guardian of entrances, Cassie had to admit. Her ear was intact and there was a slight droop to the arch under the wing of her nose but the gnawing rat had been conquered and driven out. She felt pretty sure her mother would have been satisfied with the result.

One week later, Cassie took pleasure in Dr Ryan's delight in her demonstration of how she could blow a clear passage of air the length of her left nostril and out in front of his lively eyes, just as if Ganesh had bestowed a burst of manna through his trunk into the rarified atmosphere of the surgery.

Patron of letters and learning, invoked by writers, especially poets before they begin a new piece of writing, as large as he is, Lord Ganesh can slip into any account of the power of faith to heal a rank proboscis.

*Aana means elephant in Malayalam and Anamugan means elephant-faced.

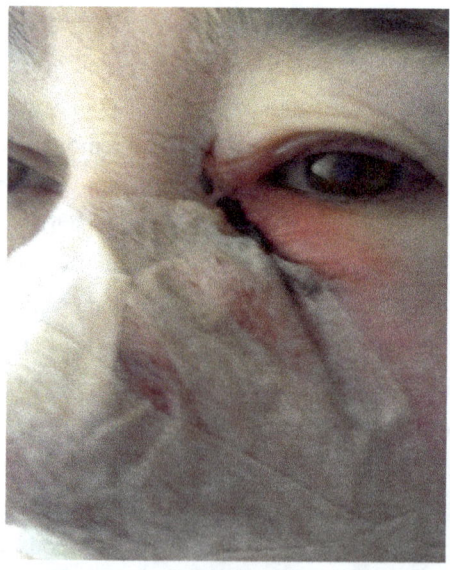

# Trust

I was the baby, the last of seven, petted and cuddled by brothers and a sister five to twenty years older than I was. Trust wasn't a concept – it was a fact of daily life.

Then one day my father stood me on a stone wall. Just five years old yet I loomed above him.

'Now, my girl, jump,' he said.

I jumped – and he caught me.

'You must never do that for anyone else,' he told me. 'I'm your father and I love you a lot. I wouldn't ever let you fall. But if anyone else ever tells you to jump, don't expect that they'll catch you.'

This was a new idea and it sank deeply into me. So! There are some people who would let me fall? Who are these people; what do they look like? How will I know them? I must remember this jump, my father says.

\*

Now I'm eleven and bumping along in the back seat of Mrs Roberts' dark red Austin of England. A few of us kids are crushed up together, our bodies touching, our thighs tingling. Jack Keegan, who's twelve, has told me he loves me and now he's putting his arm around me. This is what boyfriend and girlfriend do, I know. I've seen it before. I like him, but am I really his girlfriend? I hope not. He has my name, Jacquie. Well, kind of my name, but it's got a different ending because he's a boy. Jack and Jacqueline. Like twins. But we're not twins. We don't even look like each other. He's older than me, he's got blond hair, his shoulders hunch and he's nowhere near tall enough for me.

We spend all afternoon at Garie Beach and now I'm certain Jack will never be my twin. He's beside me all the time but it doesn't feel right – splashing in the water, and when we're lying on our towels, trying to curl his toes around mine. I can't seem to talk to Cathy or Robyn, or even shy David, without Jack butting in.

I can't breathe; he's too close all the time and I'm building a wall of air between us. He must be able to feel it. It's the length of half a ruler and floating around my arms and shoulders.

Every time he tries to grab my hand in his I flick it away. But I can still smile and listen to his stories. All about his sister. How when she likes a boy she lets him catch her. She only pretends to run fast and then stumbles deliberately, so that when she falls over, the boy falls on her. She's good at pretending, he tells me.

And then we're climbing up the cliff to the car to go home. Mrs Roberts is leading the way, along the goat track, they call it, but where are the goats? We're the only 'kids' trailing along behind, I think, playing around in my mind with highlights from my ever-growing vocabulary.

It's steep now and I'm getting out of breath. Jack and I are the last. He's in front of me. He has to raise himself by his shoulders to scramble over the edge to reach the flat land right at the top. And then it's my turn.

But he won't let me have my turn.

'Take my hand,' he says. 'I'll help you.'

I look at his hand, smaller than mine. I look at his bare chest, his arms, his shoulders. They're not as strong as my big brothers'. I look at Jack's face, his blue eyes. I can't see into them.

'Come on, hurry up.'

His hand's stretched out. I look down behind me. No-one there. Just a sweep of green grass that shoots down toward white froth on rough rocks – and nothing else but the pulsating colours of deep ocean and brilliant sky.

'No thanks. I can do it. Leave me.'

'Come on. I already said I love you. I wouldn't let you fall.'

'No thanks. I don't want you to help me. Leave me alone.' My voice is louder than usual, I notice.

\*

I never knew what the word 'shun' meant until that day. I could expect no more tingling touch of hands and thighs on the way home in the back seat of Mrs Roberts' Austin of England. Everyone seemed a bit glum, as if it was infectious.

A few years later, once I'd gone to high school, I heard that Jack had killed himself. I hardly knew him so it would have seemed strange for me to want to go to his funeral.

For all I know his sister's still alive … pretending … falling.

# Balmy Bali

He would sit on his first-floor balcony at the top-rate losman, or Balinese cabin accommodation, and sing along to his favourite song, 'When you're feeling lonely ...' He'd call out jokes and jibes to the other guests who swam in the pool below.

One afternoon, with self-conscious nonchalance, he walked up close to a young woman – a stranger who would prove to be a good listener – sitting alone beside the losman pool. She must have had a quality about her of empathy – perhaps he'd noticed this earlier in the day when she and her husband had been teaching their infant to swim. This afternoon was free time for her, with her partner and child in their room having a nap.

'Hello, I'm Gerry,' he said, shaking her hand.

'What a lovely name. What does it mean?' She thought a scrap of humour might lessen the intensity of his gaze.

'It means trouble. Trouble for Mum.'

She wondered which Mum he meant. If he was referring to his own there was a chance he'd have a few problems to relate; if he was directing the title to her, at least they knew where each other stood.

Susie introduced herself and wondered whether he even took in her name. He asked no questions, but babbled on: one day he'd approached a girl to have 'a bit of a chat' and she'd said, 'Will you can it?'

'Now that's a bit off, don't you think? It's a bit rude, especially to a stranger.'

Already Gerry had established his sensitivity; perhaps even his fragility. This was an empty afternoon and he offered a distraction for the young woman who took up his invitation for discourse.

'What work do you do, Gerry?'

'I make teeth.'

At a loss for a ready reply, Susie looked away. Then, not wanting to hurt him as the other girl had obviously hurt him, or at least he implied she had, Susie tried to turn this surprise into a positive conversation ploy.

'It makes a person stop from smiling and want to look the other way when you say that.'

'Oh, you've got nothing to worry about. A couple of tiny fillings. That's minor.'

The conversation chip moved back and forward a few times and he sat down beside Susie at the edge of the pool, his blond-haired legs extended into the water, swaying back and forwards. Then came the question that opened the floodgate of his memory. Why did he come back to Bali every year for his holidays, Susie asked?

'You must really love it here.'

'Love it?' and he looked as if she'd hurt his deepest feelings. He lowered his face, holding his head in his hands at chest level. When he looked up, Susie knew that the introductory uncertainty was gone. His eyes flicked off to the side and his voice was quieter and more solid.

'You know, I spent eleven months here, back in 1972. I was twenty-three then

and pretty naïve. You could say it left an indelible mark on me. I learnt a lot in that time.'

'Eleven months is a long time here.'

'Yeah, well eight months of it was spent in jail. I met some lovely people in jail here – you could say the most interesting people I've ever met. Americans and Balinese, mostly. Really warm people. Sincere, you know what I mean?'

'And what was that for – jail, I mean? Drugs?'

Gerry pulled his legs out of the water and turned away from her slightly. The sunlight on the pool and the sparkling droplets of water falling away from the calves of his legs dazzled her.

'Well, yes and no. It wasn't that simple, you know. I mean I carry my own shit, that's no problem. I've got some dope right here in my pocket now. That's okay. It's Bali. This was different; it was a frame-up. I know that because I found out later. I know who did it. If I'd known then what I know now ...

'You see I'm different now. I changed a lot in that year. When I went back to Australia it took me about two years before I could get into the swing of things. You know, a routine. I kept thinking everything had changed, that everyone had changed. I remember going down to the pub with Dad. You know, we had a couple of beers and then he said he was off home, and I said, "No, I'll wait a while".

'And I did, and I felt so sad. And then it hit me. It's not everyone else who's changed, Gerry. It's you who's changed. You're the one who's different. Because I learnt a lot here, and it had to have an effect on me. I cried that night to think that I was a different person. But what could I do? I'll tell you how it happened, if you want to hear.'

Silent assent from Susie. Who could refuse?

'It was very different in Bali back in 1972. You know, all of this street was just bare. There was nothing here then except a juice bar and an eating house right down the end, at the beach at Legian. The juice bar was run by a girl called Made, yes, another Made. There are mostly only four traditional names here, as you've probably discovered. Made's juice bar. I'd go over there from Kuta every night on my bicycle for chapchay. I'd already been here about three months when one night she called out to me as I rode past in the dark.

'"Ger-ald," she called out. They all do that with my name for some reason. They stress the 'ald' part. So I stopped and she said to come in, that she wanted to tell me something. So, okay, I went in. I liked her. But I didn't go over there every night just to see her. I liked the food, mostly, and I was a young twenty-three, you know, the middle son and Mum's boy, but no wimp or anything like that. I knew what it was all about, but still, I was pretty naïve, as I told you.

'Anyway she had a proposition for me. She was an orphan, although she had plenty

18

of aunts and uncles, and other family, and a grandfather, and they all lived on the flat behind the beach. But she owned the land, she told me. It was ten acres. And the deal was for us to marry. She'd provide the land and it would take $7,000 to build a losman for tourists and a private section for us, our kids, and the pigs. And all I'd have to do is marry her. Well it was a compliment, really. I should have taken it as a compliment and left it at that. Balinese marry Balinese. But they don't mind a bit of new blood every now and then, I thought. I mean, think of it. You'd have it made, right on the beach. When Dad found out later he said, "If only you'd let me know at the start." The money wouldn't have been a problem for him.

'So there I was, twenty-three, and this was what Made was putting to me. I said, "Well, that's all okay, Made, but you don't love me."

And I went back outside and got on my bike and started off, and she called out, in the dark, "Ger-ald."

So I stopped, and with my bike underneath me, I turned around and said, "What Made? What now?" and she said, "Ger-ald, you're a gentleman."

'Well, that knocked me for six, and that was it. She softened me right down,

because I'd never been called a gentleman before. You know, you imagine being called that in Australia.

'So we settled on it, and we went to formally visit her grandfather. He took me into town to see about having building plans drawn up for $7,000, and Made and I went off on our honeymoon. Because that's the way the Balinese do it. They check out whether the chemical reaction's going to be alright before the wedding. It's a good idea really. Or that's what they told me, at any rate. If it hadn't been alright I wouldn't have gone on with it. But it was beautiful. We stayed in the hills up near Ubud and it was just beautiful. You know, not constant sex – just when we felt like it. And it was just good to hold onto someone in bed every night. That's important, I think, a kind of balm. It restores your balance, knowing someone is just content to be with you.

'Every couple of days we'd come down to Kuta for a surf and Made would carry my surfboard on her head, on top of her bag, the way they carry baskets. It was unreal. I mean whoever heard of their girlfriend carrying a surfboard on her head? It was too much. I should have known it was all too good. I knew, but I didn't know. And I was outmanouevred.

'There was this guy down at the beach who had his eye on Made. You know, all that land. Not a foreigner, a Balinese. I know him. I found it all out later. I could have handled an Australian, or even an American, but a Balinese had it all over me.

'So there I was walking back from the beach one day and they grabbed me. Found the dope on me and by the next day I was in a stinking hole of a jail in Gianyar. It was just a cell, really, and so old … it was built maybe three hundred years ago.

'It was tough and I nearly died in there – from the food and conditions, and the fear, most likely, but I lived through it all to tell the tale. Thirty days I was in there, and I couldn't get word out to anyone, my family or anyone. I was so sick I thought I'd die. And I can remember when it rained I'd press my face against the bars and yell and scream I was so frightened. You know, I suffered from claustrophobia – I had done since I was a kid. I yelled and screamed as hard as I could and no one came, no one took any notice.

'Made came to see me. It was pathetic really. She'd pedal the fifteen kilometres and back to bring me food, because the food in the lock-up was stinking. The only other person who came to see me was a Baptist minister. He'd been living here ten years and only had one real convert, he said. Which I think is understandable – their combination of Buddhist-Hinduism takes care of all their needs. It suits them. Anyway he got word out to my Dad, and I took notice of what this man told me. I didn't take notice of anyone else but I took notice of him because he was a very principled person. You know, you could tell he was very strong, morally. Some people, you can just feel that about them. Very strong.

'After I'd pleaded not guilty, been sentenced to eight years jail and was appealing, he advised me to plead guilty.

'He said, "Look, Gerry, eight months is eight months, but you know these people, they could hold up your appeal for two years and you'd still be in jail." So I dropped the appeal and they sent me down to the jail in Denpasar. It's not there now, that jail, but it used to loom large in the minds of the local people, it was so tough there.

'And Dad got things moving. He contacted the doctor who'd delivered me at birth – he was a backbencher in Canberra a few years later. Dad landed over here in his fancy suit. He's sixty-four, my Dad, but he looks fifty. And he saw the Director- General of Prisons – he was a military general, you know, with brass buttons and stripes on his epaulets and all. Dad wore his best velvet suit with brass buttons too – this was the early seventies, remember – and when the secretary outside the Director's office saw Dad, he was impressed. You know, Dad can be very charming. When he went into the office, the Director-General, or whoever it was in charge – there are levels and levels of bureaucrats – he looked up from his doodling – because you know, that's all they do all day, that and lunch and inspections – the guy stood up and said, "Can I offer you a seat?" Dad and I laugh about it now.

'So it worked out that I lived in the grounds of this bigwig's house which was attached to the jail. I taught his children some English and they taught me some Indonesian. I was allowed out three days out of seven, after a while, when I could be trusted, and I'd come down surfing to Kuta. I smoked dope, just the same as before.

'One night I was late getting back, and the place had guards all around to stop the prisoners getting out, of course, and I went up to the gate and banged away, trying to get back in.

'It made me laugh, the irony of it. There I was pounding the gate to get back into prison. I'm thumping away and the guards are asleep or something, smoking, and out of it maybe and they didn't open up for ages.

'Bang, bang, bang, I'd go. You know it was like they were deaf or didn't want me back. And I had to wonder why I wanted to get back in so badly. The difference between heaven and hell is in your mind, I reckon.'

To Susie this stranger had seemed like a nerd at first, and as his story developed, a victim wanting sympathy. But in the space of a few minutes Gerald had turned into a philosopher extraordinaire. There was no need for her to offer him her sympathy, after all.

What he required was her respect – and he'd earned it by living through an initiation by fire into Balinese culture, his journey past purgatory and back, and his extraordinary narrative of that trip. She was sure of him now. The tenor of his voice, his body language, these convinced her she'd been privy to a deeply-felt account of Gerald's personal heaven and hell, his singular discovery of the 'doors of perception'.

Susie's silence, a smile that showed her gleaming white teeth, and a gentle nod of recognition, were enough to satisfy the story-teller. He had nothing to add.

She made her way back to the losman and her sleeping partner, to her role as inmate in her very own prison – in contrast, a prison of love. Back to the very balm of a loved one's body held close, a pleasure that Gerald had known so briefly – torsos locked in gentle embrace, allowing only temporary protection from a very uncertain world.

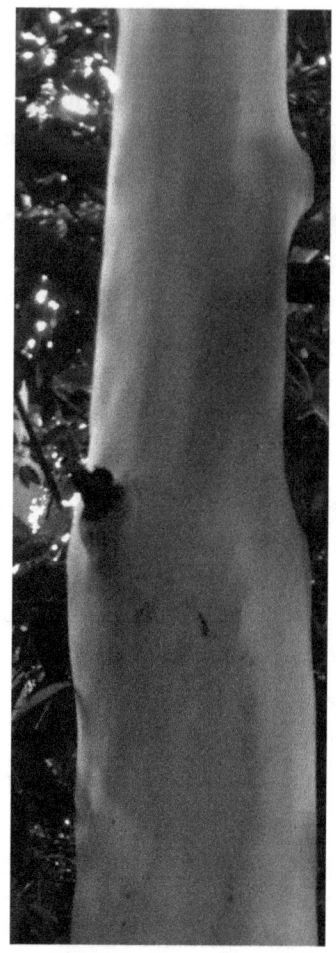

## Mother Earth – Father Land

Maria liked to tell a story about how when she was twelve and her family were evicted from their last rented home in Sunderland, her father ringbarked the trees in the landlord's back yard, out of spite.

As the story goes, he had quite a bit to feel spiteful about – he was forty-one, supported a wife and six children on a tradesman's wage, had been hardworking all his life, and owned not a stick or stone you could call property.

Even as a child he'd earned his keep, tramping through the bush hauling sugarbags of native flowers he'd picked to sell at the station or the entrance to the cemetery to make some extra money for his mother. To make ends meet, she also grew double white chrysanthemums, dahlias with heads the size of pumpkins, sweet william and sweet alice planted in pairs for romance, and daisies of every sort known locally, all for her son to sell in the streets.

Her husband, Redmond, or Red as he was known, was a drunken legend in the town, drinking his winnings from a golden casket over the period of a couple of years. He had a fifty-four-inch chest and was so strong he once carried a dead heifer, carting it off a railway track using the brute strength of his arms and massive chest and back, to clear the line for trains.

This man was arrogant and cruel by all accounts, and used his mind, which was sharp when not steeped in alcohol, to sharpen the wits of his children. They would hide under the house when they heard him coming home at night. If caught, they might have to recite the wording of a new sign erected in the town that day. God forbid if they hadn't seen it, or that they might have forgotten one of the words or even how to spell it. Their father taught them two rules for life: be observant and trust no one. It was best to keep out of his way most of the time.

With no worldly plans for his daughter, Olive, the old man had great ambition for his working class sons, and they rose to the pinnacle of all the trades at that time, as 'technically advanced' electricians. He chose singular names for them all, then nicknamed them: The younger boys were given royal names, Edward and Henry, changed to Teddy and Harry, and the older boys were in order: Earlstone, who became 'Lordy'; then Lincoln's name was shortened to 'Lin'; Alwyn was known as 'Ali', or 'Alligator'; and the fourth son was named 'Ulysses' after the ancient Greek warrior, shortened to 'Ully' with an extra 'l'. He was given a middle name, 'Gresham', which must have had a stylish ring to it. Full marks for foresight. This son, Ully, would live up to the high ideals set for him. But rather than engage in war, by the time Ully had reached the age of forty-one he'd set quite some distance between himself and his bullying father. There was no love lost between them.

\*

Maria loved her father Ully in the spirit she understood him – in a proud self-righteous way. Many people loved him, each in his or her own way – he was a big man with a faithful heart.

Even after his death when he was nearly eighty, Maria bore some of the emotional scars he'd suffered. In some misrepresentation of the Bible, she believed the sins of the father's relatives weren't worth a turning of the other cheek. She could share the bitterness she felt on his behalf with her younger sister, Julie, who would act as a sounding board, not daring to openly challenge this embattled view of their father.

It was years after the death of Ulysses, and soon after the death of his brother, Lordy, that Maria went to visit Lordy's daughter, Pattie, the only cousin Maria had kept in contact with. After the visit, Maria described to her sister how easy it had been to stir up a pot of bad blood with their cousin over events long past.

'It was probably a sensitive time to say anything, so soon after Lordy's funeral, but Pattie was going on about how she must be careful about "tying up the will" so there would be "no loose ends" in case she lost money to her step-mother,' Maria explained.

Lordy's second wife had left him years before, and Pattie had looked after her father when his diabetes became so bad he couldn't get about. Then, after he went to live in a nursing home, she visited him every day.

'Pattie was telling me her step-mother didn't deserve anything, and I agreed, but I couldn't contain myself, with all that gossiping over his money, so soon after he'd died,' Maria went on.

'And it wasn't only Pattie. Everyone at the funeral had an opinion. His money! I put them all straight about that!'

'What did you say to Pattie about that?' Maria's sister, Julie, ventured a neutral question, knowing that their father had suffered financially as a result of her grandfather cutting her father out of his will – and well aware of the unfairness of the decision.

'Well, I said that I'd rather she didn't talk about the will, because it was a sore point with me since it had been the cause of a split in the family years ago. She didn't know a thing about it. So I told her straight.'

'The property you're talking about, I told her, was purchased from the sale of land in Sunderland that originally belonged to my father, and is still rightly his. Grandfather Red bought it on conditional lease, but that was only after my father had given it to our Grandma Alice. He didn't give it to Grandfather Red at all. When she died without a will, Grandfather took over the land and gave a block each to all his children – that is, all his children except the rightful owner of the land, my father, your Uncle Ully.'

'And how did Pattie react to that outburst?'

'She said that she'd wondered when she was young why her father and Dad never had any contact, and her father had said that Ully had always wanted to go his own way. That he liked to hold a grudge. I laughed out loud at that, but we let the subject drop. The atmosphere was too sour.'

But Maria hadn't been satisfied to let it drop completely, without an even stronger impact made where it fell. Soon she was off to the Land and Environment Department to find out the facts.

She discovered that their father, Ulysses, took out a lease on three acres of land in 1936, a lease due to expire in 1947. But in the first year of the lease he transferred it into his mother's name, Alice Anne. Ully wanted his mother to have that land so she'd have some security for the first time in her life, and wouldn't need to put up with her husband's abuse any longer. From their baby bonus, Ulysses and his wife paid for a house to be built for his mother. He helped build it, in fact, because the baby bonus soon ran dry. As a licenced electrician, he was able to carry out all the electrical wiring, and as a jack-of-all-trades, much of the carpentering and plumbing, wall-lining, window-fitting and flooring as well.

Alice still had some of the younger children living at home with her and was grateful to her fourth son for the fine roof over her head.

About this time, Ulysses had a falling out with his father and a couple of his brothers who were working for less-than-award wages. These were the politics of The Depression years.

Alice Anne died intestate in 1943 and Ulysses' father became the administrator of her will. In this capacity he was allowed to take over her lease and purchase the land for sixty pounds. He then had it subdivided into eleven building blocks, selling some for ready cash and giving a block each to his daughter and five of his sons.

Also about the same time, Ulysses, his wife and six children were being evicted from their rented house situated across the railway line from the rest of the family. The other side of the tracks.

Ulysses was desperate for space but couldn't afford the rents being charged in Sunderland. So he took a morning off work and turned up at the Lands Department's head office in the city, looking for another opportunity to lease. This time the bureaucrats offered him seven acres of bushland on the highway ten miles from Sunderland and a couple of miles from shops and public transport. Familiar with bushland around the town, Ulysses decided to take the lease, to immerse his family in the pleasure of living close to nature.

He built a house in haste over a period of two months. The family moved out in stages, matching the progress of the construction, with two of the older children, Maria just twelve and Joe aged nine, spending nights alone in the partly built house. Sometimes they perched under large coolie hats as their only protection from the rain, listening in the dark to feral dogs and cats and native possum life in the surrounding bush. The family clung to their more civilised abode in Sunderland until the final stroke – an eviction order, followed by Ulysses' defiant ringbark branding of the eucalypts.

Grandfather Red paid them a visit to look over their new property. The meeting was brief and surly.

On his death a few months later, Grandfather Red left his son, Ulysses the brave, his tools and a ten-pound note, being some misguided calculation of his rebellious son's share in the worth of the original property. Ully refused the money but took the tools.

'I suppose he needed them. He was building a house,' Maria lamented to Julie to explain away the chink in their father's pride. But what daughter could understand the psychology that binds father and son?

'What hurt Dad the most was that all his brothers and his sister accepted the old man's decision which in fact meant that they stole their brother's property. By this time, they were all living in established homes on their blocks of land and wouldn't give them up. One brother, Ali, had been living with his father and had stayed on in that house. When he died, only in his forties, the house was sold and the proceeds split between them all, once again leaving Dad out. So he had nothing more to do with them.'

'And you want to stir up the coals by telling Pattie about what happened all that time ago?' Julie couldn't help but ask.

'Yes, I do. The smoke from the smouldering coals was already intense enough to make me choke. I've stirred up the embers and I don't care how fiercely they burn, to let all the descendants know what a sanctimonious, deceitful, parsimonious lot of land-grabbers their parents were. I photocopied all the documents and sent them off to Pattie with a little note saying, "just in case you didn't believe me". I'd told her that I might go with her to scatter Uncle Lordy's ashes on the land overlooking the bend in the river they loved so much, you know, The Needles, where they swam as kids. But I've changed my mind since I found all those documents. I don't want to be involved, even though I used to feel close to Uncle Lordy in my twenties.'

Somehow Maria had lost her nerve now the relish for payback had been requited. Ashes to water, dust to fire. The blood sap of the eucalypt, oozing in thick bubbles along the gash ringing the tree's trunk, had sunk into her memory long enough to spill over the limits of death to claim rebirth.

*

The day Uncle Lordy's family chose to scatter his ashes turned to 40-degree heat and gusty winds to match the occasion. The temperate bush scene rife with sentimentality that they'd looked forward to, gave way to the shock of a scorching blast of heat in their faces as they left the protection of their air-conditioned car. Blowflies buzzed at the moisture in their eyes, sweat trickled down from under their armpits and breasts, tiny ants stung their ankles.

The man of the house, Pattie's husband, forgot his lines, and the youngest son fell and grazed his temple on an outcrop of granite, screaming for attention.

The ashes were flung in an attempt at a graceful gesture before a gust of wind rising up the escarpment whipped them back into the children's faces. Ashes mixed with dirt, who could tell the difference, body from land?

A single kookaburra reflected on the lack of fresh meat in the family's scattered refuse, laughed at the disappointment, and flew off to richer grounds.

# Pearly Shells

At my parents' grave last week, standing above their buried bodies – corpses, really they are, but I still think of them in vital visceral form – I asked them a question about love, asked from deep in my heart. Immediately, I saw in my mind an image of a shell, a spiralled conch shell. I was puzzled. The image was clear and strongly imprinted on my mind.

Today I view a documentary on numbers and their central role in describing the universe. I realise that as a consequence of humans gaining this descriptive knowledge comes an understanding that numbers must be central to its very construction.

I'm currently reading a fictional account of Galileo Galilei's life, hearing him exclaim again and again that God is a mathematician. The documentary program bears this out, showing illustrations of the exact geometric shapes on which Chartres Cathedral was built, guided by St Augustine's mathematical studies. The number pi, for instance, plays a central role not only in the formation of circles but in other formulae, such as determining the normative in a range of statistical situations. A nautilus shell is displayed to illustrate the 1.08 progression, small to large, of the rooms or segments of its shell. In other words, as the sea creature grows, each chamber of its shell's growth is 1.08 times larger than the last chamber, creating a logarithmic spiral within the exterior of soft pink stripes on a cream background. A thing of beauty.

As I watch the screen, I struggle to remember when it was that I'd received the image of a conch shell, a sea spiral, as an intriguing answer to my query about love ... and I recall my brief conversation with my parents, and then a silence, into which the image arose, almost in an instant, as if it was their personal response to my question and prayer. An image which overtook my thoughts, thrown up from the depths of a great well of knowledge.

*

So I go to my friend Google and find that shells are symbolic of the protective quality of love because they provide a strong armour of defence. They protect life and even shelter pearls. In Roman mythology, Venus, the goddess of love, was said to have been created from the foam carried onshore on the top of a scallop shell. The Hindu goddess Lakshmi was also thought to have been formed from the grit that creates a pearl within a shell. More generally, in Hinduism the conch shell is symbolic of an awakening of the heart of the faithful because it is heard by those who live with love in their hearts.

My mother used to say that her name, Marjorie, carried the meaning The Pearl of Great Price, an idea she must have picked up as a child and delighted in ever after. It's certainly an appealing catch-phrase. The name does mean 'pearl', but someone must have endowed it with even greater value for her alone. So that as a girl, and a pearl of great value, she felt safely cocooned within a craggy oyster shell — a rare artefact in a mining village, Beaconsfield, in northern Tasmania in the early 20th century. And in turn, as a woman, she nurtured her own children, the last, the seventh, named Christine after one of the greatest protective avatars of all time.

Back in their day, she and my father swam the tides of life, just as conches, alive in the sea, are swept along with their eyes, feelers and suction caps their only sense organs for navigation and security, save their strong, vortex-spiralled outer shells, pointed at both ends. Now buried in dry land, my parents can only offer me a memory, a shell of the protective love they gave me when they were alive. Or is it more than just a memory from the past they offer me now?

In Prakrit indigenous poetry in India, the conch, or shankha, often has an erotic connotation:

Look,
a still quiet crane
shines on a lotus leaf
like a conch shell lying
on a flawless emerald plate.*

The erotic effect is evoked through the contrasting image of the creamy quality of a conch shell set against a starkly green precious stone, the emerald, said to vibrate with love in perfect tune with one's heart chakra. The emerald symbolises wisdom, hope and success in love through the fidelity of one's lover.

I've read about this language of precious stones, the age-old myths of their powers beyond the scientific known; I feel I am swept along by these swirling unconquerable currents of nature let loose to bestow good fortune, extending further than anything our conscious minds will ever comprehend or control.

Like a conch, the crane – a bird which symbolises long life, even immortality – is able to trumpet the future using its distinctive call. Since the meaning of Shankha is beneficence and bliss-giving, in Hinduism the sacred Shankha shell is used in ritual as a ceremonial trumpet sounded to begin worship. The warriors of ancient India also blew 'divine' conch shells to announce battle, hoping for a cleansing auspicious beginning to drive away evil spirits, as described in the famous epic, Mahabharata.

Hindus depict the preserving aspect of God, or Vishnu, holding a conch, a Panchajanya, to represent life, in the belief that it emerged from an ancient churning of the ocean, which produced the nectar of immortality. This divine shell, Shankha, is praised in Hindu scriptures for bestowing fame, longevity and prosperity, and as the home of Lakshmi – the goddess of wealth – who is Vishnu's consort. His very own pearl. The legend is an acknowledgement of the power of female sexuality. Remembering that each human life originates within the body of a woman, arising from the secret of erotic desire.

And I learn that the Shanka, symbolising water, has always been linked with women's fertility and serpents or nagas. Without any embarrassment about such symbolism, the southern Indian state of Kerala has taken this shell as its emblem, perpetuating the former emblems of the Indian Princely state of Travancore and the Kingdom of Kochi.

Finally, I find that a Shankha shell crushed into powder is used in Indian Ayurvedic medicine, for stomach pains and also to enhance its 'pearly shells' – beauty and strength. Who would dare doubt these reputed powers? Surely, only a miserly unromantic sceptic. I'm a willing believer.

I discover that, in fact, many different kinds of molluscs can produce pearls. Even the conch. So my mother's message is gaining more and more credence. Pearls from the Queen Conch, Strombus gigas, are rare, having been collectors' items since the Victorian age. Conch pearls range from white to orange or even a pale brown, but pink is their signature colour. They have a unique attraction, a silvery, iridescent effect known as 'flame structure', caused when light rays interact with infinitesimal crystals on the pearl's surface, also said to resemble French moiré silk, or the quality of the surface of running water.

Now, skimming through my precious, still scant research, this time in sacred Western annals, I find that The Pearl of Great Price is a significant story in the scriptures followed by devout Christians the world over. In the New Testament book of Matthew, Jesus is said to have told his followers a parable titled, 'The Pearl of Great Price', about a merchant who is searching for beautiful pearls. Finding one pearl 'of great price', he sells everything he owns so that he can afford to buy it. That pearl is 'the kingdom of heaven', a great treasure indeed. The reason the pearl is considered to be symbolic of the kingdom of heaven is that the story follows on from another parable, through the use of the word, 'again', about the conversion of St Paul, who was said to have unintentionally found the hidden treasure of the kingdom of heaven and given up everything for it.

My mother must have felt the thrall of the pearl, as she even identified herself through two mother-of-pearl brooches, one the shape of an 'M', the other its reverse, a 'W' – her initials – that she used to wear, set against a black suit jacket for dramatic effect. Aligning oneself with such an irresistible, universally-acknowledged romantic image as the pearl would be a deeply-satisfying pleasure, I can see. And now I feel sure that this message of love and protection has come from her to me, as if a whisper from the sea heard through a shell held to the ear.

My mind floating in a world of creative reverie, I too feel an urge to consciously identify my love with the symbolism of the conch shell, since that was the exact image I saw in my mind's eye as a message from both my parents – whose inner shells, the bones making up their skeletons, lay buried beneath my feet.

After all, I've dived deep into the known facts of marine science, able to describe the conch and its almost priceless pearl, as well as plumbed the mystery of the shell's universal symbolism and as metaphor. What need is there for me to quest further? I'll go with the flow. Bob along on the waves. Yes, in a conch that might carry a passenger safely, traversing an entire ocean before reaching her destination.

This is a sacred message my mother and father have bequeathed me as a comfort in my distress, settled as they are in a single grave after more than eighty years of husbanded fidelity. A signal to bide my time. So that I, like St Paul, may give up everything – outworn material dependence, cramped emotional attachment – once the time is ripe. At Vishu, perhaps, the first equinox of the zodiac year, as a golden cassia showers her petals in a downpour, like tiny canaries swooping to carpet the earth in colour.

A sign that I will find a treasure, and dwell within a spiral of perfect symmetry, a kingdom of love. Perhaps a living conch – there must be some male shells, surely – may even wash up on my foamy scalloped shoreline one day.

---

*Hāla's gāhā sattasaī 1.4, tr. M. Selby. From a collection of 700 single-verse poems by more than two hundred poets translated from Mahahashtri Prakit dating from the time of King Hala (c. 200 BCE to 200 CE).

# A Footnote on Footlights

As Sri Devi and Jack find their seats in the cinema, the lights go down and in comes a couple who sit the other side of Jack. Sri Devi doesn't see the man until later because he's sitting on the farther side of the pair, but the woman is noticeable. She must be feeling cool because after a minute or two she picks up from near her feet a black leather jacket that she's placed on top of her bag. She unfolds the jacket and puts it on. About twenty minutes later, once the main feature has started, Sri Devi watches the woman put her right foot, her foot closest to Jack, up on the back of the seat in front of her. The foot is bare, with red painted toenails showing starkly as a contrast against her pale skin, in the faint light thrown from the cinema screen.

The foot comes and goes from Sri Devi's view as the film, a political comedy, picks up pace. Sri Devi has her arm snuggled along Jack's underarm and midriff, as is usual for them at the cinema … until some dramatic point in a film when she often snatches back her arm into the psychological safety of her own body's heat.

About halfway through the film, Jack slowly moves his right leg to cross over his left, balancing his knee near Sri Devi's thigh and extending his left sock-covered foot so that it's a smidgen away from the woman's bare foot. Sock-covered? Since when does Jack take off his shoes in public – or even at home for that matter? When he's going to bed, is all, Sri Devi thinks.

So there they are, those two odd feet: one clothed in a sock, a male white sports sock with a red cap covering the toes; the other a bare white-skinned female set of toes, displaying a red cap of nail varnish. Both distracting in contrasting red and white, viewed from within the darkness of the low shifting light of the big screen.

Sri Devi knows this surge of feeling within her so well. Some long-forgotten spasm of fear that another woman's sexuality has caught the attention of her lover. A dormant feeling sprung into primitive life again, that familiar vice of jealousy searing her senses.

How many times has a similar scenario played out between them over the ten years they've been living together? Sri Devi knows she should have adapted to Australian society by now – recognised and accepted the dominance of men, their tough emotional distancing when matters of commitment and loyalty are raised, their individualism, their male mateship – but her South Indian background serves little use in these harsh emotional circumstances. She only has herself to blame, she thinks, being so blinded by her attachment to Jack, smitten by the enthralling quality of his cavalier behavior and his exotic culture. He was her first and only lover after she left her family and home culture to study in Sydney. In going her own way, believing she was an independent person in a new age of opportunity, her experience of the support of her powerful mother, matriarch of an extended family back home, had proven so little use to her now.

Sri Devi consciously tries to clear her head as she feels the blood in her veins rush with heat. What to do? Will she sit out the movie, distracted by thoughts of footsie, by imaginings of the thrill of an electric arc between bare bony flesh and cotton polyester garment? She tries to play with words such as 'podiatric poaching' and 'toe-ing and fro-ing' to distract her passion, with visions of rising instep under fallen arches. Now she grasps at her thoughts, which are attempting to make a calculation of the fraction of space that separates the clothed from the naked.

To take stock of her mind Sri Devi takes stock of the sock. Leaning across Jack's chest, she swiftly grabs his toes, holding them firmly.

'Why aren't you wearing shoes?' she asks in a level voice. The woman's naked foot whips back into darkness, recoiling with speed as if from snakebite.

'What?' Jack hisses as he glares at Sri Devi, his leg suspended horizontally.

Still leaning across him, 'It's just that I wondered why your foot and this woman's …' she whispers, maintaining a monotone.

Jack turns to face Sri Devi, who momentarily touches his chest and feels its pounding to match her own, as the other woman slinks down in her seat, hidden now behind Jack's rage, and the man leans over the woman to find out what is going on in the dark.

A dense black fog hits Sri Devi's chest and her mind simultaneously, as if bursting from Jack's body in a shock wave. An ugly overpowering black fog, it penetrates Sri Devi's rib cage in a flash, invades her heart as poison, seeping through to its centre, then sweeping along the veins of her chest and arms, pumped through her body as adrenalin, even surging into her thighs and calves. Then, in an instant, her overheated blood has turned to ice.

'What are you saying?' Jack's voice rasps.

'I just wondered what was happening,' Sri Devi croaks, her head, her thoughts, her weakened voice faint yet clear above the frenzy inside her, now turned frozen and fractured, a weight in her lower body.

'Nothing's happening.'

Jack and Sri Devi stare at the screen while she struggles to concentrate on its large and noisy characters. After a few minutes she tucks her arm back along Jack's, surprised that it's accepted. She's decided to make light of the episode and use Jack's raging body heat to recharge her own body temperature, through a façade of 'making up'. Over an hour later, as the credits roll, Jack directs Sri Devi outside with a curt, 'Shall we go?' He indicates the direction of the exit further along the row, turning his back on the couple. He's steering her away from any unseemly incident, she realises. No time to savour the film and check the names of director of cinematography and best boy, as the lights come up.

Outside on the footpath a torrent of words gushes from Jack's mouth. 'Oh no, my girl, you won't be able to pass this one off, not this time. Let me tell you, I feel absolutely fucking furious about what happened in there. What the hell were you doing? What in God's name were you on about, making accusations about me in the middle of a movie?'

'I would have been happy to discuss it then and there, Jack, but what's the point now? It's over.'

'Okay, so I'm used to scenes in public where you seem to have absolutely no regard for anyone else and just start screaming about whatever delusions you have at the time. But there was no way I could deal with it then. The woman's husband must have thought you were stark raving mad. What's this mad woman on about, he must have thought?'

This is the first time Sri Devi has had the thought that Jack might have been scared that the man could react violently and make a physical assault on him, there in the cinema. This possibility hadn't entered her thoughts, until Jack now points it out. Clearly a very male reaction, and part of the male psyche, she sees. She had been oblivious, she now knows, and this realisation causes a little crack in the walls of her ego, to think that she could have underestimated someone who seemed to have a minor role in a situation and overlooked his possible reactions. Not that that would have stopped her, anyway. But she won't let the walls protecting her ego burst now … won't allow herself to indulge the floodwaters of her emotional self and be pushed to launch a detailed accusation, to be intimidated into creating a dramatic scene with an uncertain result, especially not here in the street, where there is no evidence of any wrongdoing, when some of the main characters are dispersed and all is now in the realm of the memory.

'It was hardly a scene, Jack. I just wondered why you had your shoe off.'

'What sort of accusation is that? I mean what did you think was going on?'

'It's not an accusation. It was a question. But it's over anyway – and we can't relive it now.'

They're already at their car, parked very close to the cinema entrance tonight. Sri Devi takes out her keys. She has to drive, as Jack had a bit to drink earlier in the evening. Into the front of the car from opposite doors, they move in rhythm. Now, silence.

She turns the steering wheel, and accelerates as she swings the car out into heavy traffic.

'You're driving like a mad thing. Watch these people – you'll hit someone,' Jack directs Sri Devi, as if he's in control of both of their lives and fateful actions.

A policeman on a large brown horse, looming above Sri Devi's soft-top sports car, is attempting to control the stragglers from a crowd emerging from a nearby football stadium as they dart across in front of the traffic.

It's dangerous here, Sri Devi thinks, as she cuts back her speed and decides this is no time to inflame Jack further by rejecting his overbearing driving advice fired at her inches from her face.

Silence returns and lasts all the way home.

Now in the kitchen, Jack is whistling and fondling the cat as he tries to project a feigned invincibility … as a prelude to a second blast.

'I want to say again that I'm very angry about what happened tonight. I've been falsely accused many times in my life and in this case the accusation is laughable … just preposterous. And I want an apology.'

'What accusation? There's no accusation,' Sri Devi tries to cut in.

'Let me finish. I haven't said even one tenth of what I mean to say, whether you like it or not.'

Before the raving gets under way in full voice, Sri Devi pipes up that she's got something to say too, once he's finished.

And so Jack's ranting takes over: about Sri Devi's insane jealousy; about his innocence in flirting; about her exhibitionism in public; about her complete disregard for other people's feelings.

When he's finished, Sri Devi says that she's sorry that he's so angry. No, that's not enough, he says. He wants the accusation withdrawn. But there's no accusation, so how can it be withdrawn?

'It wasn't dealt with at the time so any attempt to bully me now we're at home on our own is not really going to change that,' is the stroke of brilliance Sri Devi puts forward as her next gambit.

A faint expression of self-doubt flits across Jack's eyes and forehead. Bullying: now that's a new word in the jaded vocabulary of their verbal wars. Shaky ground for him, perhaps? Sri Devi can see he wants to think about her interpretation some more, in the hope of refuting it later.

'What do you think? That I was trying to seduce that woman by rubbing her foot with mine? I'm not such a fool.'

'I'm not saying you consciously set out to seduce her. Perhaps it was an unconscious response to her.'

'Oh, so this is the great 'cover-all-situations' claim now, is it? Unconscious. And if I was acting unconsciously, don't you think I would have quietly touched her higher up her leg, groped her thigh in the dark, maybe, as it rested in the seat beside me? You wouldn't have seen any of it. I'm not so stupid that I would have touched her foot stuck out there in the open, where you and her bloke could have seen it all, am I? Am I that stupid?'

Well, no, he's not stupid, but IQ is not a major factor in the workings of the unconscious, nor of the male sex drive, particularly after a few beers. Sri Devi thinks this but dares not say it, out of fear of further provocation. She's alarmed that the hypothetical scenario has taken an unexpected turn with visions of even more groping in the dark than she had imagined.

'And I think I deserve … at the very least if you won't withdraw the accusation … that you say you're sorry. Sorry for the public mess that you and your insane jealousy and wild imagination create, over and over again. It's just another typical example of your madness and self-centredness and I'm supposed to put up with it, am I? Well, I want an apology.'

'I've said I'm sorry you're so upset, and that I've caused it. What more can I say?'

There's quiet. Not a full deadly silence but a quiet after the storm. A stand-off. Sri Devi won't say a word in case she disturbs this passive interlude, which may lead on to a sweet and settled calm. She hopes just such a gentle quietude will follow, as it has on other nights, if the battle lines can be ignored long enough for a truce to emerge within the bounds of domesticity. Sri Devi is thankful that she has had to give so little ground.

She moves her arm slowly towards the refrigerator door, opens it, and takes out a soft-drink. She reaches out for a glass and pours Jack a drink, a routine for him before bed. He turns away, heading for the bedroom in the hope, she thinks, that he'll soon find release from his rage in peaceful sleep.

Sri Devi is tired. So tired. She checks the medicine cabinet and finds a small bottle. Lethal. In one swift movement she pours a few drops into Jack's drink then takes a gulp herself, before carrying the glass through to their bedroom.

As the couple lies down to rest side by side – on their backs instead of their usual singly-entwined, twinned-foetal, spooning position – they each wait for sleep to restore their own and the other's harmony. Clean knocked out. Not a word spoken. What's there to say, and how many more times could she possibly suffer the playing out of such a pathetic drama, Sri Devi thinks?

She can only hope that sometime during the night their souls may reconnect and lie in unison, as their bare feet petrify into cold alabaster by sunrise. Then Devi Durga Shakti, the all-knowing all-powerful warrior goddess, may swoop down upon them, clutch them in any number of her eighteen arms, and career away with them beyond the darkness, so that together they may merge into an infinity of space and light.

# Smoke Dream

My daughter, Natalie, aged sixteen, had a dream about Elvis Presley and James Dean. She has a poster of James Dean on the back of her bedroom door, so that's understandable. But Elvis? She doesn't really know much about either of them. No question that they have reputations for being sexy, though.

In her dream, a woman reporter was explaining the stars' personal lives to her and others in a group. The reporter would say, 'This is James Dean's toothbrush,' and he would be standing next to her in his home, and would agree. He'd nod. Similar for Elvis. Was there any coincidence that her mother is a reporter, I wondered?

This morning she caught the bus into town to meet Vicki, and I think she told me she was then going to see Jessica about an interview for a modelling job that Jessica had been lucky enough to snare. But I'm not sure, because I didn't really want to pry, and only insisted that Natalie not stay out late, because I wanted her to study later in the day.

'Yes, Mum.' That oh-so-bored, 'what a pain it is to have to listen to her nagging,' tone was obvious. She had to meet Vicki at 10.30 at Central station and went by bus.

At a quarter to twelve she rang and explained that Jessica had gone in for the interview-audition for a dance tour while she, Vicki, and another friend called Diana, had stayed in the waiting room for a while because Jessica was nervous.

The reason she was nervous was that Diana had gone for the same audition on Wednesday and it had been bondage-style. There was no photographer or video operator there in the room that Diana could see, but the interviewer had asked Diana to wear a leotard and chains and roll around on the floor, hanging onto his ankle while he held a whip.

Yesterday Diana and a couple of her friends had told their very prim private ballet teachers in their sixties about this. The teachers, the Misses James, receive lots of requests from commercial companies for their students, and all that they had suggested was that the girls could phone a few advertising agencies to find out more about that particular firm. They were ingenuous. Natalie didn't use that word to describe them; she said they didn't take much notice.

Today was Sunday, just four days later, and Natalie was worried because Jessica had gone into that audition room alone while she and her two friends had waited in the next room for ten minutes before Jessica had come out to speak to them. She was shaking and she told them that they had to leave the building, that they should go for a walk, and that she wanted to get through it all in about half an hour. If she was longer than that they should start worrying, she said. So they left the building, but after the front door slowly eased shut, they realised they couldn't get back in again.

Natalie had rung me after about three quarters of an hour. Could I ring the company, Sydney Commerce Corporation, Natalie thought the name was, because none of their phones were charged? Could I say I was Jessica's Auntie Natalie and I needed to speak to her urgently? Ask her questions to which she could answer, 'Yes' or 'No,' to find out if she was okay.

I asked if Jessica would want me to do this.

'Yes, she was shaking when we left,' Natalie said.

'I'll drive in as well, do you think?' I asked.

'Yes please, Mum.' Suddenly this is the voice of a little girl, not the young woman with a cute façade of sophistication that she usually assumes. She gives me the York Street address of a multi-storey building.

I try the number. No answer.

I try again to be sure and let it ring. No answer.

Okay, shoes on. I tell Jack, who is engrossed in a football match on TV, that I'm just going up the street to visit my mother for a bit. I can't phone the police because I assume Jessica's parents don't know she's having an 'interview' – and, after all, I don't know for sure that she's being molested. And she's gone there willingly. But if the girls can't get into the building, I won't be able to either. Would I be standing helplessly in the street, waiting for Jessica along with the girls? What good would that do?

Phone the fire brigade, is my first thought. It's a stroke of brilliance that has just jumped into my mind. I've never before in my life called the fire brigade, because I've never been in a fire. But I presume they know how to get into buildings. Even skyscrapers!

Soon Natalie phones back and I tell her, 'No, the Commerce Corporation's number doesn't answer. I've called the fire brigade, so if an engine does arrive, maybe you might walk down the street a little, or maybe speak to a fireman, whatever you think.' Mixed advice, I realise. I'm almost as flummoxed as the girls.

Drive very carefully in the rain into the city, is the sage advice I give myself. Then I drive the length of Clarence Street, one way, before I turn and begin with the early numbers of York Street, one way.

I see a fire engine – oh, I should say I see fire engines. Plural. Count them – 1, 2, 3, 4! And men in uniform all over the place. What have I done? Four fire trucks! Appliances, that's what they're called, I tell myself, trying to take in the enormity of the trouble I must have caused!

The girls look even more worried than I expected. Who wouldn't be? The door to the building, a new office block, is open, with fire fighters inside and out. The girls are gathered on the opposite footpath about thirty metres away now, staring at the multi-storey building as if expecting someone to jump through a plate glass on a suicide dare. I pull up sharp and jump out.

'Go up,' I say to Natalie. I don't think there's any use in my going into the building, as I have no idea where the audition office is, and my car is propped in an awkward parking spot, half up on the footpath.

'No!' A look of fear and shame.

'I'll go, then. Which floor is it?'

'12.' Natalie has been reduced to monosyllables.

'Is there a fire here?' I ask the first couple of hard-hatted men I encounter. 'Do you mind if I go up to the 12th floor?'

'Ask the man in the red hat,' I'm told.

'Do you mind if I go up to the 12th floor?' I ask him.

'Well, we've just been up there, and we haven't located any fire yet, so that should be okay. There are people still in the building.'

I move to press the lift button.

'You'll need an elevator key,' he says.

So I stand about while the firemen work out how to get a key to the fire stairs. There's no smoke, and the red hat with the kindly face looks at me curiously.

'I'm waiting for a friend of mine,' I tell him. 'There's some sort of bondage thing going on up there. ... Have you seen a young girl come down?'

'A girl came down a few minutes ago. That's how we went up in the lift – using her key.'

Back to the car.

'They say that a girl came down a few minutes ago.'

'Jessica hasn't come down, Mum.'

Back to the firemen.

'Is there some sort of party going on up there?' the same fellow asks me.

'There's no smoke. ... Do you think there is a fire? ... It seems a coincidence. ... Strange, isn't it?' I manage to throw out these attention diverters to put him off track. I sound as confused as I feel, though my confusion is not about what he most likely thinks it is, a fire.

Just then, Jessica walks out of the lift, wide-eyed, or at least acting so. She doesn't seem to understand what I'm doing in the foyer. What does Natalie's mother have to do with all this?

'The car's outside,' I say.

'Do you need to go up in the lift now?' the head fireman asks me.

I walk purposefully towards the red hat, touch the solid workingman's hand, say, 'Thanks very much,' look into the surprised eyes and briskly leave the building.

*

I've been through a one-way 'discussion' about parental trust of adolescents with Jessica once before, only a couple of weeks ago, so I'm not about to go through the 'lecture from Natalie's mother' routine again.

In the car I can hear denials and declamations coming from the back seat, which I studiously ignore. These girls with beautiful lithe bodies, children's faces and electrified nervous systems. Innocents abroad and a danger to themselves, I think – but don't vocalise.

'I think it would be best if you just come home now, Natalie, don't you ...' I say, using a statement tone rather than questioning.

There's general agreement we'll all go to our separate homes.

Of course, I'm filled with guilt that I've called out so many firemen. But if Natalie was in such a scrape I'd want someone to do the same, I'm sure of that. One engine would have been quite sufficient, though. It's the very most I expected.

I'm a little nervous that there might be a follow-up phone call from the Fire and Rescue Service and I know there's no way I could lie about what happened to save my skin.

When we get home Natalie makes herself scarce and I retire to my bed to contemplate whether during quiet periods at work fire officers ponder philosophical questions such as 'Without smoke there's no fire,' or 'Risk management is a telephonic form of emergency containment'.

Months later the promised dance tour for Jessica has not materialised. Who's surprised? I guess the only problem for her will be when she's a famous movie star and some reporter from a dirty rag uncovers an old porno film of her in sexually compromised poses. But come to think of it, this may only add to her public appeal. And that's what counts these days.

Let's hope she remembered to clean her teeth.

# Black Magic

Two facts only, Jack knows about Sasha's trip.

One: her ostentatious hat with feathers, black and cream. She'd worn it at her gallery opening, with pearl necklace and earrings to accentuate the line of her neck.

'Will I take it?' she asks, wanting to stay on safe ground with travel advice.

Pains shoot across Jack's face. 'I don't know, Sasha. I only know I love you.'

Of course she doesn't take the hat with her, once she sees his mind's hellish picture of why she would want to wear it – for someone else to admire the bony upper vertebrae leading to her hair tucked under the feathery cap.

Two: Jack knows that she'll be going to a Grateful Dead concert in San Francisco with her lover, Paul. Yet it's Jack who should go, to relive sexy sixties nostalgia.

The two facts will merge.

*

In the dark of the Grateful Dead concert, amid the crush of the packed audience, the stark contrast of black and cream appears in the form of a woman. She has long blonde hair and wears a black bowler hat. She stands in front of the couple, Sasha and her lover Paul, as they cling to one another.

The woman slowly moves into Paul's tunnel vision. She hooks his eyesight. Or he hooks hers. Minutes pass as a black thread of sex inevitably pulls her backwards, swaying, stoned, closer ever closer, waiting for his touch.

Hers are snaking movements, side to side. He swivels his hips too, compelling her towards his sense of touch.

Denim-covered penis beckons denim-covered arse. She backs up, moving to the music's beat. He is smiling. The sound of a rock guitar riff wraps around them all in swirling blue and red lights.

Denim to denim, they touch at last.

Paul puts his arm around Sasha's shoulders, close beside him. His body is harmony. Hers is stiff, hard, cold rock. He tries to pull it toward him. It doesn't budge. At last he feels the blast of wind with ice-needles. Raising his hands to protest his innocence. 'Where has she come from?' he mimes, muted now, cooled and cautious.

Sasha's hands sweat, her heart pounds.

Still the woman swivels her body, blocking the band out of sight, the music out of hearing. Nothing exists but the black hat and blond hair with its mesmerising power.

Sasha can endure this until its end, she thinks. She waits, like a cat on a raft in swirling rapids. Her breathing is shallow and controlled. Her mind races to find a way out of the drowning sensation, the flooding through her body of a red sea of rage.

Fighting through to some consciousness, her thoughts find a solution – then comes a warming of her heart from the energies released by memories of a hot country far away. The now red rage running through her body subsides as golden honey moves from her mind down her throat and spreads through her arms and chest. She grows stronger – no longer a shell being pounded from fearsome outside currents, but filled with solid flesh and bone, sinew and gristle.

No need to endure anything at all, even for an instant, Sasha thinks. She need not stand by to observe.

She pokes her right forefinger into the small of the back of the cream-and-black body. It sways and the head swoons. Sasha jabs again. The figure turns to show off a smile. Sasha's mind sends out knives from her eyes, swords from her hands, fire from her mouth.

Fear on the stranger's face and then the back-hunched body moves off. It bends its back, with weakening knees, collapsing into a cross-legged heap on the floor. Not once more turning to look. The spell is broken.

Sasha takes Paul's hand to touch her ribcage, to feel her heart pounding through her chest.

'Are you alright? It's racing,' he says.

Racing, she thinks. Across thousands of nautical miles to the safety of Jack. Pulled by a rope plaited from his thick, black, wavy hair. The plait begins its journey into the abyss of darkness, falling down that familiar long, strong man's back. It moves with speed, snaking across baked earth towards a golden seashore, skiffing across the ocean's sheen, sliding through endless waves, flanking dolphins and carbuncled whales, sinewing past bright brittle corals and shining starfish, sounding the depths of the seas, until at last it echoes its way into the showering noise of the great concert hall, moving – deft and smooth – past swaying, vibrating bodies into the darkness of music to seek out Sasha's labouring heart.

Her chest is aching as it struggles: away from a cold black night's moonlit cavern of mistrust filled with crowding, milling teeming bodies fleshed and painted for the underground sensation of sex; towards the day's sundrenched womb of fidelity and a haven of hope.

Sasha has been charmed from afar as the night's power wanes. The rock music winds down. The lighting loses its exotic brilliance. Everyone looks normal once more, back to the activities of real life: finding animal comfort and shelter for the night.

Sasha will wait the night out, the days out, in secret. She knows enough to flood her heart with blood. Thick and red, it gushes from her wounds. There's no need to speak her suffering, to call across the land and sea. It is lodged unspoken in two other minds. Her knowledge is sure.

Never again to risk caring so much. Never again to risk, caring so much.

The part of Paul's mind that is hers spills over into his conscious world. He tells Sasha that he took over one of her dreams in his sleep. A young woman loved him but he showed little interest.

'Everyone's dreams are their own. You dreamed it, not me,' she responds. She cannot let his thoughts seep through the tidal cracks in her scaly shell of silence to steal her pearl again.

*

Weeks later he writes to her about another dream: 'A woman dressed in black with blond hair. I beckon her. "Come closer," I say. She slides down in front of me; her legs give way. And I see she is a doll. It must be you. Come closer. The dream is true.'

'Dreams are true for the dreamer,' she replies on crisp airmail paper. 'I don't have blonde hair. Mine is black and long enough to plait.'

What she doesn't write is equally true: too much sex weakens the knees and strengthens the mind.

Dreamers may keep their knowledge hidden. Wakers must rouse themselves to find it. Only the grateful dead can move between two worlds.

# Anticipation

When Christina arrives at the literary conference at Montague University she finds her name is booked for two rooms. As both her surname and Christian name are not unusual she believes that there must be another person attending the meeting who shares the names.

'No. No-one else is registered by that name,' the receptionist confirms vaguely. That's strange.

'So you have a choice. Would you like ground or first floor?'

'First floor please.'

To ease the burden, as Christina ascends the winding wooden stairs on foot, a load of books she's just picked up at a sale over one shoulder and an overnight bag weighing down her other side for balance, she imagines an alternative scene, West End London in the 1920s and a dapper lift valet swanning her aloft to meet her lover for high tea in the midst of glass-walled chintz and art nouveau.

But as she reaches the top stair, a darkened corridor leads her along to what she finds is the wrong keyhole. The receptionist must have given her the key to the other room, on the ground floor.

I'll check out the downstairs room anyway, before I take the key back, she thinks, hoping for an idyllic alternative. So many prosaic choices – where was the romance in life these days?

Downstairs she swings open the door to find a 5pm-winter-lit, under-cliff interior. As Christina creeps through the doorway her skin also creeps along her backbone. There's one small window for light but the view is of a brick wall, which would angle the world away from her rather than open up her life to full sunshine and a spacious vista. She shudders, knowing she'd made the right choice first time.

It's only as Christina wends her way back to reception to explain the error over keys that her mind flashes: the ground floor room, Number 56, was the other Christina's old room when she was resident at the university. The invisible other Christina, the shadow writer/mentor tangled through her own inner life, has resurfaced. Welcome back, dear one, she thinks.

Christina ponders the usefulness of trying to explain the visitation to the receptionist, and attempts a jocular observation but it goes unnoticed. Reception and organisation have blocked the receptionist's ears to literary references.

With this prologue it comes to pass that Christina wonders who it is she is representing at the conference. Sharing a first name with such an eminent writer, how much does she represent herself, journalist and biographer, and how much her deceased subject? Which hat will she wear tonight? She's brought only one as it happens. She's never worn it before but hopes to do the other Christina justice at their common book launch. They're interdependent and Christina the biographer knows the routine of counterpoint almost by heart.

At the opening of the conference on the first night, Mary Knight, who will launch Christina's book the following day, is very agreeable to her. What a contrast! The last time they met, Mary had kept her waiting at least half an hour in an anteroom, disregarding of the agreed appointment time. Mary now explains that the interview was difficult for her to give as she still misses her close friend, Christina the Major.

The next day Mary is back at the conference, with a blond grandson who breaks a glass, spilling lemonade on the floor, a sign Christina the Minor takes as fortunate. Mary calls out a pet name to a man with wide shoulders: 'G'day, Shoulders.' Mary and Christina the Novelist had both been able to pick out a good sort. A second glass is broken by an onlooker as Christina the Biographer takes the stand. She thinks she must be doubly lucky and touches her hat, feeling grateful that she was bold enough to wear it, allowing her a role-play for protection.

Mary says Christina's book is the first and best. Everyone laughs, knowing another biographer is slowly working towards publication.

Christina the Postmodern reads her speech and then an excerpt from the work of Christina the Late and Great on the subject of hats … reference to the Paris setting, to elegant fashion, to 'savoir faire'. The stuff of romance the Christinas share.

At dinner there are two seats vacant. Christina knows her shadow, Christina the Incomparable, is sitting opposite her, unseen, while another eminent literary figure sits invisibly opposite her very own golden-haired biographical boy. Another so-far-unpublished biographer gets the seating mixed up, and is parked opposite a lachrymose poet.

After dinner, back in the conference hall, the winning parody for the night is based, as everyone can guess, on Christina the Unconquerable as Games Player. The author of the parody is a biographer too, and just happens to share the name of Christina's father, David, so perhaps he is not quite himself tonight. These ghosts of biography can play nominally clever tricks with identity. It's hard to see what hat he's wearing so Christina loans him hers to accept his door prize.

As she leaves for the night she notices the man with wide shoulders. She thinks that's all she sees, but it's possible he has blue eyes. They're non-committal, she can see that much. So she acts out a trifling flirtation. Just a brush of her fingers across the milliner's plumage; a glance to the side. Wearing such a hat, it's important to be noticed – for the sake of the hat, of course. She can't be sure she's had any effect on him.

The next day the man with massive shoulders embroils himself in a lover's triangle, perhaps unwittingly? Christina alone watches his discomfort grow. He swallows hard twice when the guest speaker, an attractive woman of eligible age, will not let him off the hook in their public debate over a literary pedantry. He has to call out as he is speaking from the floor, whereas she has the benefit of a microphone. He is sitting behind the guest speaker's lover who turns to stare at him, to stare him down. 'Shoulders' towers above the guest speaker, who stands on the stage dwarfed by the tiered benches surrounding her, and her resentment over his questioning is acted out in bold feminist style as she hurls his imprecise statements back at him. Verbally he retreats, but Christina hopes that the blend of his mild manner and powerful shoulders hides a deeper manly passion. The other Christina would have swooned within, she guesses.

A few nights later Christina goes without her wedding ring to the conference dinner dance, hoping nervously to sit near his shoulders. It's the only body she's interested in, although others hover about. She finds there's a fine camaraderie at her table, as well as the shoulders, opposite and two along.

Does the alcohol make him oblivious, or does he see danger, which causes him to turn away? He's friendly but non-committal to the women about him. Nonchalance, Christina wonders? One woman is persistent and he takes direction from her impassively. She pulls him to the dance floor. His rhythm is flawless, his stature commanding; by contrast, his partner radiates exuberant tension completely out of time to the music.

Christina longs to dance with him and dispense with these hand-pumping plodding-footed dancers she has to lead. But he won't ask her to dance. Has Christina ever before asked a man whom she longs for, to dance? Never. She has asked men she doesn't care a whit for. That's been easy. But she's never before asked a man she admires. He will not ask her to dance, she's sure of it. He always replies to her conversation openers but never initiates.

They must be lovers, Christina surmises, after an hour watching the woman's close, longing looks. But no, he's a clean-living family man, she's told. The woman is one of his PhD students who's had too much to drink. This is not what Christina sees, however. She sees that he enjoys the attention but does not commit. He wants to be pored over, clung to, but he makes not one move that might incriminate him. He wears a ring on the second last finger of his left hand.

Christina's chest is pounding as she leans across to him during the single moment the woman is distracted from her amorous possession. Christina has put a lot of thought into the question she will put to him and she phrases it in a way he cannot refuse. He cannot, she believes, since she calls on the one passion she knows they have in common. They are both students of Christina the Powerful. Christina, weak now, follows the question with a statement and a nod of the head:

'Would you dance with me? One for Christina's husband.'

The husband's name is the same as his of course. So they are an historic couple. Christina and Bill.

His only answer is a physical affirmative as he takes her arm, and then they're up on the dance floor together.

But already the woman is causing a scene, pulling at his shoulders, turning him away.

Christina can't believe this lack of grace, this physical tussle. She has never fought over a man, and here, the first time she has ever asked a man she longs for to dance, there is a public scene. She is not wearing any hat at all, but she can't be the same woman she has been all her life. Which Christina is she, after all? Men ask the Christina she has always been to dance; she doesn't ask them. Surely this is not Christina the Magnificent's experience. If the cap fits … No, it's the wrong size for them both.

So this is what happens when a woman openly competes for a man, Christina realizes. She's astonished.

But the uncivilised scene is being smoothed over so quickly. The man Christina was dancing with earlier steps forward to ask the disruptive woman to dance, to avoid any unpleasantness. The woman can't refuse. She stares at them from the arms of her new dancing partner, a wildness in her eyes.

'Shoulders' is incomparable as a dancer. He is a prince of movement compared with any other man on the dance floor. This is the jive which Christina cannot dance adeptly because she missed out on learning it in her youth, a few years short of the baby-boomers. At first she feels gauche.

But what unfolds is the perfect moment in time. She knows it, because her gaucheness doesn't seem to matter at all to these shoulders. He says, 'This one's for Christina's father', and then, challenging her eyes with his own, 'This is a test of your power of anticipation'. They are above the ground, dancing as smoothly as if she is waltzing – a dance Christina is familiar with - but with more pace and excitement. He leads her so that she never takes a false step. As if he's a magician in spats, he turns her apprehension to soaring confidence and she realizes that she must do only one thing: anticipate. She must feel what he wants her to do. She finds she has a hidden talent for it. She concentrates only on him and what he wants her to do next. The bond is timeless; it is bliss. She has never danced with a man who is so attuned to the rhythm of the music. She follows him, in anticipation.

When the music stops the woman is claiming her possession again. Christina and Bill are no longer floating. They stand, feet hard on the floor. The woman's eyes glare at Christina. Bill mooches away. Christina's earlier dancing partner, the gallant fellow, takes her arm.

Just before midnight Christina is hot and takes off her black jacket to reveal her backless dress. Is it in reaction to this that Bill straightaway stands up, when his guardian is absent for a few minutes, and makes a movement to go? He leans across to Christina and says, 'Okay'.

It has the sound of defeat.

Does it mean he admits that, after all, she has had an effect on him? Or does it mean that he acknowledges that his behaviour with the female student is not blameless for a religious family-man? Christina wonders whether she has sent him that message or whether it is still her secret thought. She has been watching him so closely while she talked and danced with other men, and he must have known that she was watching him throughout these rituals. Perhaps he anticipates what she thinks, instead of the other way round.

Or does he simply think he's had enough to drink and should go to bed while he is still clear of complications for the night. Christina wonders, though, whether he is so religious that he has to leave before the midnight toll turns him towards debauchery. She tries to anticipate, to imagine him praying in his room, but can only see him doing a pee.

She is left to puzzle over what this 'Okay' meant to him. For all her life she will wonder. Having begun to anticipate his thoughts, she finds she cannot stop.

Christina leaves the dance soon afterwards and, back in her room, cries hard, stretched out on her bed. She doesn't need him, she knows, as she will return to her faithful, lusty husband the next day. Not a great dancer, it's true, but dancing's only for parties, after all. Still she wonders about the sensitivity of those shoulders. Academic language can mask only so much feeling. The way his throat looked when he swallowed, in interrupting the guest speaker, had revealed there was mutable flesh and pumping blood behind the dilettante's mask.

When her passion was exhausted and the exquisite ache of tears had subsided, Christina put on her ring again. Come daylight she could resume her marital, material identity in a way the other Christina could not at the end of her life, as she was without a loving partner, holed up in cramped university accommodation which was offered at the whim of a breed of 'critical professional' she deplored. The flies around the honeypot. The prevaricator's curling vines around the artist's fecund figtree. Academics passing judgement in recommending writers for residencies.

Christina vows she'll try a broad-rimmed style next time, an elegant sunhat with a burgundy velvet bow, to keep the sun from burning her sensitive skin, as it pours in through the windows of her room, open to the sky.

*

Christina, back in mother and journalist mode, would have liked to meet her elusive dancing partner in the street sometime. A casual hello and a smile of goodwill would have satisfied her by default. When she did see him, months later, at a fruit market, she was wearing a backless top. Curious, she thought. She wasn't in the habit of exposing her back; in fact she hadn't worn a backless top since the conference dance. And rarely before that. Is this what attracted them to each other – back to back, receding into the distance? Could they neither face each other nor commit their imaginations to their own fiction? He had seen her flesh and bone at the dance but she had not sighted his spine, she realised, so perhaps he didn't have one.

There was no way she could tell if he had seen her. Now in the midst of the market crowd, he was just a middle-aged man with a slight jowl, out shopping with his two daughters, she thought. He lifted the box of fruit and vegetables onto one shoulder to carry it to the car. She wouldn't have thought it was so heavy it needed to be transported this way.

When you hear a man whistling you know there's something up.

# A Green Thumb and a Lotus Hand

We sit cross-legged and face-to-face sideways on the old marble steps of the ghat lead-ing down to Lake Pushkar. The morning is misty, foggy. Smoky is what it is, from the villagers' woodfires.

    'Please be comfortable, and we will have one ceremony. I am honourable priest and you are very lucky to be here in such temple to Lord Brahma. It is the one only Brah-ma temple in the whole of …'

    '… India.'

    '…in the whole of the world! It is most sacred place …'

    'But Varanasi and the Ganges …?'

    'Yes, Varanasi, the Ganges river, these are sacred. But this is special only Brah-ma temple in the whole of the world.'

    'Yes.'

    'We must begin. I will be pouring water into your hand four times and you will pour again this water four times into my bowl. Show me now your right hand.'

I extend my open palm.

'So what is your good name?'

'Christiane Taylor.'

'Where are you coming from?'

'Australia.'

'Now we will pray for all that you need. Please take some pleasant water in your right hand and …'

Without warning, my right earring given me by my youngest daughter falls from my earlobe into my lap.

'That's my daughter, Jessamina.'

The slightest look of puzzlement crosses the pundit-priest's mainly poker-faced expression. A young man, so many years my junior, he has a face at once soft-featured and strong, a benign quality the overriding impression made on me. There are no sharp edges to any of his facial traits. Across his forehead, a broad banner of white ash in three horizontal slashes adorned with a red central dot strikes into my vision, as his dark eyes directly and deeply engage my own.

'Will I put the earring back in?'

'Yes, please to go ahead.'

For once I don't fumble, and the earring slides back into the hole of my right lobe easily by touch.

'Now we must begin.'

'One, two, three, four,' we count, as together we concentrate on the success of this initial phase of the ritual, the pouring of water into a small metal bowl.

The young pundit tells me to take some water in my right fingers and cleanse my ears, nose, mouth, eyes – plus my forehead, 'for your good thoughts,' he adds.

I begin with my earlobes, thinking of Jessamina's health, and her presence here with me in the fall of my earring. After moistening all my five sense organs, I find I'm touching my crown chakra. But too soon, it seems. I haven't followed the instructions exactly.

'Now, again, more water, and wash your top of head and heart.'

So I repeat the brushing of water across my head's crown with damp finger-tips, and burrow beneath my winter jacket to get as close as possible to my heart.

'You see that I am honourable priest. I have one sacred thread,' and the young man pulls the length of white string tied around his torso up to the collar of his shirt, so it frames his collarbone, to show his credentials and proof of integrity.

*Not necessarily foolproof,* is the thought my sceptical mind keeps to itself. For the first time, his eyes break contact with mine. Perhaps he has the power to read my thoughts, or maybe he's just responding to the tears he sees arising.

My chest cavity is welling with emotion since my brief walk with another fine young man, a guide with a gentle manner, through the Brahma temple in the twenty minutes before being set down before this obviously innately powerful young priest. The emotion had been sparked first by an older priest exchanging my mix of roses and marigolds for a full complement of red roses; and then by the sight of a Shiva lingam and a golden Ganesh figure at the very core of, the base within, the Brahma temple; and finally, by my double-sounding of the temple bell there, effected twice since I'd misunderstood the direction and pushed the whole bell instead of the heavy clapper at its centre.

I suppose, though, the emotion had been welling even longer. I hadn't wanted to leave my family and come away alone on this three-month study trip to India, to lecture at a university in the south of the country and to research a book. I felt I was too old for the hardship and life lessons always so confronting in India. My husband (a variable concept, this, since we've been together nearly thirty years but have never married) … my husband had told me he'd travel with me, but changed his mind immediately my study grant became a reality. He had every right, I supposed. So he'd opted for material comfort while I faced flagellation of my soul once again on this seventh trip to the subcontinent. I knew that, as always, I might expect both agony and ecstasy.

A few days before this temple encounter, while I was staying at a breathtakingly-beautiful palace hotel in the middle of a mystical lake, my heavy heart had begun to swell, providing relief through a spontaneous release of tears. I'd indulged myself with an overnight stay in the 7-star hotel since it was my second visit to remote Udaipur, I could never expect to return, and it was just two days before my birthday. The tariff cost hundreds and hundreds and hundreds of dollars. I blanched at the rashness of my decision (or seeming rashness – I'd suffered hours of agonising uncertainty before I took the financial plunge, hoping my husband would consider giving me some part of the sum as a birthday present).

Why me? Why am I so fortunate, I ask myself, in the midst of the palatial splendour? The quality of the experience is palpable, unable to be resisted. Not devoured greedily, but savoured. I find that all my senses are satiated, to a state even beyond saturation. The sight and sensation of being on a treasured island surrounded by a sun-sparkling expanse of water; of being in a realm of luxury of body and mind: to have my feet massaged by ripples of water on the lake's sun-gleamed surface; watching ducks take off in flight and pigeons wheeling as a body, past tessellated white walls set against the midblue heavens; inside the palace, to inhale the perfume of jasmine and tuber roses which waft along marble corridors inlaid with floral designs; later, to capture the aesthetic of a flautist perched on a walled rooftop courtyard at sunset, keening his love to the darkening sky; at night in a lush garden, to behold a graceful dancer, spot-lit, her full skirt alive with shining peacock colours and, as she whirls, a huge voluptuous shadow cast on the whitewashed wall behind her, imprinting on my mind.

I'm overcome by this beauty – and that it's for myself alone to relish. I feel blessed, ecstatic. This gratefulness releases my bonded heart as I try to distract myself by concentrating on cricket scores and menu prices.

That was days ago, but now, immersing myself in the Pushkar ghat ritual, my emotion has again begun to seep up from my heart valves and trickle out from between my eyelids. Sadness is not the cause. This is a second blessing.

'Now repeat after me: OM.'

I repeat the sacred sound, hoping to voice it as softly and lovingly as I have heard the pundit utter it, the 'O' a rounded 'A-U' sound, the 'M' reminiscent of the bond between mother and child, his lips so lightly and warmly extending the captured vibration.

We've begun a journey in song and action and I, so willing a partner, dance the steps carefully as he gently guides me along.

'Lord Brahma …'

'Lord Brahma …'

'… I give my praying …'

'… I give my praying …'

'… to ask your blessing …'

'…to ask your blessing …'.

My voice is hushed and croaking slightly and my tears gently flow as we proceed majestically through so many aspects in the nurturing of my being. A cool breeze stirs against my bare lower back so I use my left hand to tuck my jumper into my jeans. It's my only distraction from the intense concentration I apply to the ritual song. Through our mutual focus, we encompass my body's good health and protection from harm both from behind and from the front, which seems somehow to be linked with the past and future.

I, a figure who so often has her head in the clouds, hadn't ever really thought about being attacked from behind, but at least now that ground has been covered, I realise. So clever, really, to initiate a fear and immediately provide a service to alleviate it!

Coincidentally a gong sounds close beside and a little behind me, and an ancient purohit, his forehead also painted with an ashen sacred symbol, bends low as he negotiates the steps beneath me, this action emphasising the reassurance of safety given.

'So now you will have good blood, strong body, open heart, will live one hundred years. Take more water in your fingers, please. Do you have husband?'

'Yes,' I bark out, dispensing with any doubts I might have had about legal niceties.

'What is his good name?'

'Derek McDermott.' Does he notice that this is a different surname than mine, I'm wondering? But there's no pause or questioning.

'Repeat after me: Lord Brahma ...'

'Lord Brahma ...'

'... I give my praying ...'

'... I give my praying ...'

'... to ask your blessing ...'

'... to ask your blessing ...'

'... for Derek McDermott ...'

'... for Derek McDermott ...'.

We're off again on a passage down the ages, on a road well-trodden over thousands of years. Derek's body and soul are given a thorough rejuvenation, and my tearfulness eases as I concentrate on the ritual. Our voices, in delayed unison, are increasing in volume and confidence. Next we move onto the subject of other dearly-loved ones.

'Do you have children?'

'Yes, two daughters – and two grandsons, so far.' Now that he has me including the past in my welfare, I'd better take out some insurance on the future, I'm thinking.

The young man frowns, and I realise he doesn't like the way my mind jumps ahead.

'But first the daughters, before the grandchildren. What are their good names?' his voice forceful, as is my response. I chime their names, 'Natalia and Jessamina,' the sounds skittering across the surface of the lake.

By now I've become single-minded enough to say 'prayer' when he says 'praying', but immediately regret this egotistically-independent self-expression, a reflection of my purist devotion to English-as-language-supreme, or imperialism in speech. Even so, our magnificent carriage of calling-out maintains its buoyancy, its purposeful rhythm and its sedate and graceful manner of delivery, as determined by my guide's refined bearing.

Next come my beloved grand infants, Jack and James, their names offered in celebration to the Lord Brahma for safe-keeping here on earth.

'Now your parents. Are they living?'

'My mother is.'

'What is her good name?'

'Marjorie Taylor' – loud and clear, then emotion breaking through as I think of her great age and weakened state, now aged ninety-four and cosseted in a nursing home. Yet here she is, coming along with us in this glorious 'sounding ceremony'.

'Is your father dead?'

'Yes.'

'What is his good name?' Present tense, I observe. Presumably the result of poor grammar - or a belief in life everlasting.

'Hector Taylor,' and I become aware again, in this calling-out, that I carry my father's surname, not my husband's. I'm sure we would pass over this minor bump on the high road without pause, except that my voice is cracking again as the pressure in my chest rises.

'Stop crying now,' I'm commanded.

'Yes.'

'You must not cry now because your father feels this. He tastes tears, and you do not want to upset him. He needs one big full belly of delicious food so he can pass into heaven now.'

I visualise my father's fulsome belly, and my tears, with their pathetic dribble, cease abruptly, from shock.

We repeat the routine as if my father is standing right there beside us. Once, a couple of tears push over the rim of one lower lid but I brush them away quickly in case either the young man or my father sees them and becomes distressed. The now-joyous carillon completed, 'that must be it', I think.

But no, there's a pageant of people still to come.

'You know I am honest priest. I did show you my sacred thread, yes?'

'I know.'

'Do you know how many temples are here, in one such holy place?'

'One thousand!' I'd learnt the figure the night before from a guide book.

'One thousand temples plus one hundred and fifty-two residences, all around our holy lake.'

I scan the edge of the lake which is flanked by poor-quality stone and concrete buildings with little boxy windows, bare of any vegetation, not a tree in sight, not a blade of grass, no lilies on the water's surface, not one lotus petal to be seen. No green fingers at work here. Nor even green thumbs. I think of my garden back home, by contrast a veritable paradise.

Here, barrenness prevails, even though the lake was created from a fertile gesture, a toss of Brahma's hand, which sent a single lotus petal flying. As he flicked his wrist in irritation, the petal from the lotus held in his right hand fell to the ground and a watering-place sprang spontaneously from the earth, forever after to be called, 'Push-kar', or 'Flower-hand', in Sanskrit.

In 2008 the place looks bare and neglected, the houses unpainted - hardly a nosegay for the Great God of Creation. Lord Brahma had two wives, a legend I've been told by the charming guide. The two volcanic peaks that surround the lake, Savitri and Gayatri, are named after them.

As the story goes, Brahma flew on his swan to Pushkar to perform a sacred ceremony, or holy sacrifice, at an especially auspicious time. His consort Savriti, daughter of the sun, kept him waiting, so, feeling irritated, Brahma married Gayatri after that one powerful flick of his lotussed wrist. Splendid Gayatri also had some relationship to the sun. She was either one of the seven horses of the sun, a hymn to the sun, or another name for Saraswati, the mother of rivers and lakes, and more significantly, mother of the Vedas, of all learning and eloquence. Maybe Brahma was simply singing a hymn for the sun to come out to bless his sacrifice and Gayatri, with knowledge, cleaved to him. All three - the sun, flowing water and knowledge - might seem very different, and separate, entities to most people these days, but the names Savitri, Sarasvati and Gayatri are interchangeable in some ancient stories. What's in a name? What's in a wife? Brahma was the Great Creator and he had to get on about his business of creativity. Perhaps he had a lot of writing to catch up on. In any case Savitri was righteously jealous. She became so enraged by the conduct of her husband in taking a second wife, she punished him, declaring that this temple would be the only one in the world. The other Gods, Shiva and Vishnu, might have as many temples as they liked, all over the place, but Brahma would be confined to one alone.

Hearing this story, I'm thinking that this legendary squabble somewhat diminishes the boast of the temple's unique standing. What's going on here? I don't really understand the symbolism or import of this story, or what it means in my life. Two wives, three names – I've had two husbands, neither legalised. Is there a third, a consort of learning, who is waiting in the wings, ready to confine me to a temple of knowledge? Alone and far from home, I'm confused.

But the young priest intones on ...

'One hundred and fifty two residences ...'

I was born in 1952, I'm thinking. Everything's about me here and now, during this session, isn't it? $1+5+2=8$ or $1+9+5+2=17=8$, I'm calculating fast.

'...and you can see they're poor, very poor. Every visitor pays what they can. People from all over the world ...'

Earlier, the guide had spent great energy pointing out the silver coins embedded in the temple's marble stones, and its tiles engraved with visitors' names, one even from Spain, to impress on me the temple's value.

'Some people so rich pay thousands of lakhs, some pay less. You see five fingers on one hand ...'.

Well now, that was an old trick my father loved to play on children. How many fingers on your hand, he'd ask? No, not five, just four and one thumb! But, after all, that's just splitting hairs – or fingers away from thumbs – and it's mean-spirited of me to think it in this situation, I know.

'I don't understand about the hand and fingers,' I say. 'Tell me again?'

So now I'm getting the message, and can only sit and admire this proud young man's lecturing of me on the sinfulness and greed of the First World, without using post-colonial terminology, instead turning to the language of barter.

'Little people pay one thousand rupees – or less,' he says, first tapping his little pinkie's nail, then tapping the ring finger, then the next, right along to his strong, brown domineering thumb.

And the richest man can't pass through the eye of a needle, or some such, I'm remembering.

'So what will you pay for donation? All people here must be fed. You must see them, very poor.'

'Do I pay you here?' I'm wondering at this sudden mercantile turn of events in the midst of our prayerful outpourings.

'You make promise here and payment there,' he says, pointing to the top of the ghat steps, 'at one temple office,' which looks more like a wire cage with a table out front.

'Okay, two thousand rupees.' I've been doing a quick calculation based on several factors: what I think I have handy; how rich I feel; my admiration for this young man's technique, as well as his power and certainty in his profession; and finally, my glowing heart which has been cleansed by the shedding and then stemming of my tears. I too feel powerful, made fresh and new and strong by the priest's tender protection.

'Is that all you pay?'

'Yes.' Silence – and then I concede an explanation. 'It's a long way to come here, you know.'

He nods. 'Does your heart feel light?'

I turn my gaze away from his face this time, to mentally weigh my heart. I allow my thoughts to float about there in its secret, sacred chambers, checking the quality of their buoyancy and lightness.

'Yes.'

'So now we come to donation paid to me for one ceremony. I have no wife, no children, I live for Brahma, I give blessings. How much will you give?'

'One thousand rupees,' I say promptly.

A slight reaction passes behind his eyes but I can't tell if it's disappointment or satisfaction. Most likely it's a slight excitement. Surely this is a grand sum. He couldn't expect the same amount as I'm giving to all the anonymous poor people in Pushkar that he's evoked. Conjecture is useless, however, and these thoughts are momentary. His demeanour has been even and calm, a true invocation of goodness throughout, and although I'm a little surprised that the financial phase of the ceremony has been incorporated into the ceremony itself, I'm not unhappy that he's pushed me to dispense my worldly gains more widely and deeply than I otherwise would, unprompted.

'And does your heart feel light?' A repetition of the enquiry, and this time I realise it's the original version of the perennial question that comes at the end of any sale by barter throughout the East, the satisfying conclusion for all parties: 'Are you happy?'

I make another mental check inside my chest, more quickly this time, as I'm feeling confident about the avoirdupois.

'Yes. Do I pay it up there too?'

'To me, here, is good.'

I'm hoping that I have enough cash in my wallet, otherwise it's such a rigmarole to open the money folder I carry at the bottom of my voluminous bag. I take my wallet from the bag, which has been resting in my lap, between us, throughout the ceremony, and, remarkably, I find a few hundred and then exactly three one-thousand rupee notes. I pass one to him and he gives me a smile and nod. There's no hint of obsequiousness in his expression, for which I'm grateful. Not a touch of either charm nor malice. A smile for a job well done and a soul saved, two minds at ease, and my body rested from nervous strain.

Then he distributes onto a metal plate some of the flowers I've brought, points out the rice grains again, and a splash of turmeric. I see the colours orange, yellow, pink and red set against white - the variety, the plenty represented in one small dish, as he transfers a portion to the small bowl of water.

From the plate he takes a yellow and red thread and carefully ties it around my left wrist, telling me seriously that when it breaks I must leave it either in water or a tree. I frown, thinking this action may determine my place of death, yet asking instead how long the thread will last before breaking, which is a silly question, I know - and he simply repeats the instruction.

Passing the plate to me, he says I must make a praying, a wish sent to Lord Brahma, that will occur as I throw the melee of colour, the produce and flowers into the water of the lake.

'Please, do not throw special plate,' he advises.

I look at the water to judge the distance and then chuck the plate's contents swiftly and neatly – wishing, wishing, wishing.

Next, the small bowl's contents must also be thrown down into the lake, so the waste is not left with him. I must throw it away; I must throw for him. This is just a little trickier to execute since the bowl is filled with water and I want it all to reach that great shining expanse, the sun-drenched lake, not to spill onto the steps between us and its edge. I hoik the bowl's waste and not one drop spills before hitting the water's surface.

'Oh, so strong,' he declares. A mutual admiration society, it seems …

Up we stand together and he accompanies me to the office desk set against a wire security fence where an old male official (who else?) takes the two one-thousand rupee notes and insists that I fill out a receipt for myself. The young priest points out where I am to write the date, my signature, then the figure in digits and again in words.

'Write please, "T", "O", "U", "T", "H", "U" …'.

'What am I writing?' I ask, and then it twigs. I add an 'O' before the last 'U' and finish writing 'thousand', neglecting to correct the word 'two'.

I wonder at the power of this young fellow to have me misspell my own language.

As I leave I see families of grey monkeys huddled together to keep warm on this chilly north Indian winter's day. Like statues carved from a single lump of rock, they merge as one, still and calm.

I pay the guide and find I have just the right amount left in my wallet for a tip for the driver. God-given economics.

The ritual has done me a power of good: believing myself linked to heaven and earth, expressing beneficence, the strength of my mind and heart unleashed. I marvel that this restorative celebration occurred on my 56th birthday, the eighth multiple of a seven year cycle.

*My Father who art now in heaven*
*hallowed be thy name*
*thy kingdom has come*
*thy will also done*
*on earth as it is in heaven.*

\*

It takes a little while, but soon my family-working life begins to undergo a major shift in balance, its interrelationships expanding and contracting in response to unforeseen demands and generosities. I feel I've been launched on a tiny coracle to navigate the ocean wide. Yet I feel safer than I've ever felt before. No dangerous riptides or storms ahead, behind, above or below. I'm reminded of Leonard Cohen's description of what it's like if you can escape the limited thinking of 'love as object'. Only then, love:

*broadcasts in front of you and in back of you, to the right of you, to the left of you,*
*above you and beneath you, and you're in the centre of a forcefield that includes*
*everything that has no inside and no outside, that doesn't look at anything, nor*
*does it need to be looked at. It's like the taste of honey when you're very young.*

\*

A few weeks later a couple I meet while waiting by a carousal for baggage reckon they were ripped off in Pushkar by a conman who duped them into agreeing to a temple ceremony. They felt put upon, they say, calling him an enforcer, a fix-it wallah for a panjandrum, terms I thought had long ago died the death of so many colonialists. How is it that white skin can bloat the ego and blind the senses enough to have you think you're eligible to trespass on a culture without paying a due?

Panjandrum indeed! Jessamina tells me in a phone call that her pain from arthritis has lessened. She's learned to train her mind to better handle stress, rather than be wedded to the fickleness of others' judgements of her. 'Oh, and by the way, Mum, I've been growing some petunias on my balcony and they've just burst into flower – a brilliant red,' she tells me. And she wants to know if I've been wearing her heart earrings.

So what have I gained, along with an adeptness in applying fashion jewellery? Nothing less than a godsend: the power of a clear shining mind, open to receive new blessings and see old blessings in a new light, with restored faith in love's divinity. As articulated by an honourable youthful soothsayer of an ancient world wisdom, who's taught me to navigate generously every thought, word and action in ritual. Even the flick of a wrist.

## Baisant des fleurs

She knew she was a solid citizen – mother of three, dutiful daughter, reliable senior public servant. She was strong enough for these roles, she was sure. And yet at times her emotional commitment to this grounded life that had evolved over decades would suddenly turn to water, without warning.

Rather like the time she complimented a man she'd just met on the quality of his bow-tie tying. Most men wore ready-tied bows if they wore bow-ties at all. Only a connoisseur would learn the craft of tying, are the words she used in praise of him. He scoffed modestly and their business meeting began. As it proceeded she watched, fascinated, as the movement of his Adam's apple undid the loose button on his shirt collar, causing the bow to unravel gradually, irrevocably, inevitably, to lie loose and limp below his open collar.

She made her escape from the meeting at the first opportunity, unable to bear the pathos of wondering what could be said to rescue the man's pride when the tie fell completely apart and dangled like a spindly scarf about his sorry chest.

The problem in her settled life was that she took the time to smell the roses, as the saying goes. And not only roses, but any flower in season and in perfume: violets, a song rising out of dark, dank low mulch; gardenias overblown in blowsy cream satin; geraniums, tangy, earthy and rude with colour; wallflowers hiding a fresh sweetness above their bulky green foliage; rosemary, pungent as she plucked and crushed it between her fingers; lemon-scented gum reaching her involuntary nostrils on the air.

Lately, though, she was finding it hard to distinguish between the flowers she inhaled and the men she kissed. Each experience was an adventure in sensuality, and she the ardent explorer. She didn't go out looking for blooms; they grew naturally along her path.

On her work desk she nurtured a pure red geranium growing in a small earthenware pot. In a sunny position, facing north, it flowered on and off all winter. Each time she broke off the last vestiges of blossom, she held a fear that the ageing plant would not give her a new crop. That his love would be finite; that he had given up hope.

A month or two would go by as the hardy geranium slowly formed tiny new buds, growing out of a place where a branch joined the main stem, and she would sing along its growth to full blossom. Then she knew she would hear from him again, and then fear again, hear from him, and fear, into infinity.

At home, she had taken a cutting of geranium, a branch from an old bush, and pushed it into soft earth to create new healthy stock. It was advisable to do so, since an old bush weakened and could not bear the same quality blossom season after season. Still, she tempted the balance of nature and time in nurturing the fragility of the plant in her office.

The chance had come now to transplant or take a new cutting from the office plant. Something had to be done, she knew, to shore up its contracting root system. Fresh earth might be sufficient in the old setting, for she feared transplantation to overwatered soil. Not knowing what method to use, she decided on transmutation instead, and foresaw a rose, with thorny danger to anyone who tried to steal a flower and escape quickly.

They say a rose by any other name. The red geranium had worked the adage in reverse when she fell to talking with a man of means and middle-age on an inter-city business flight. His personal name was forgettable but his family name was Wolf, carrying the same meaning as her recent lover. She hadn't noticed the common meaning of the name until she was ensconced in his hotel room, ostensibly for a drink before dinner.

During the taxi ride from the airport, her body had felt comfortable beside his, always moving to the touch of his warm entreating palms – but her mind raced ahead to deny his hopes. He described his beautiful home, his lack of wife and children. What sense of thrill had carried her along with his charming suggestive repartee?

Sometimes his cleverness outstripped hers. After he told her she could get a cheap rate at a swanky hotel where he was staying, he asked her whether she knew where she would be sleeping the night. To pause before answering would have been an admission of uncertainty and open up the possibility of sleeping with him, so she laughed and told him, 'Yes', knowing she had no idea. But she was happy to check out his hotel to see if the discounted rate was still available, she said.

Sometimes her cleverness overreached his. He asked her what her kitchen looked like and she told him she hated cooking, which was the answer to the question he'd really intended.

'Do you ever use truffle oil?' he gently coaxed. She declared she'd never heard of it and wondered whether he was relieved or disappointed that she was no yuppy, and would offer no competition in the culinary arts.

As she entered the hotel, the doorman gave her a red rose, which she proffered to the wolf to smell as they ascended the main escalator. He couldn't detect the perfume so he grumbled that it was a hothouse variety. Earlier, she'd inspected his hands to see the characteristics of medico or financier, which he claimed as his professions, and saw only rough skin from home gardening, as he explained it.

Once in his room, she found a vase in the bathroom, and was frightened to see that it was made of black ceramic, and she told him twice, for emphasis, that she was taking out its contents, clinging ivy, to place the single red rose on display. By now she was feeling a little spooked. She set the vase on a table beside the king-size bed of wolfish appetite.

Now comes the point in the story to describe the quality of his kiss. A friend of hers who had kissed her just the evening before – softly, gently, slowly – had challenged her to write about an act of love. If you could read the ecstasy of an orgasm, she'd thought, who would ever act it out? The flesh has so much more potential than a bunch of words.

This wolf's kiss is soothing, caressing, reassuring. 'Come follow me,' it calls to her, as all wolves' mouths call … at the beginning. His hot, firm, supple lips press and pull hers into his own. As his strong upper arms also close her in, she feels the smallness of his upper back. At one with each other, they move in synch. This body is not six feet tall and broad, she recognises thankfully. It reminds her of no one else. Not dominating, not demanding, and very easy to match with her own body's impulses. Once she's within his ravening arms, she feels comforted, almost as if eaten whole. All wolves fit the same, she thinks. Some with strong forelimbs, others with iron-hard thighs.

There are many interruptions which keep her safe from complete enthralment. A plumber must be called because the shower won't turn off. Water running down the drain and out to sea for want of use worries them both. Another time a waiter knocks and brings in Thai chicken with pistachio nuts, begging Mrs Wolf's pardon for the interruption. She wonders whether it's worth the effort to scorn the waiter's sly aside with a denial of the role of wife. Then comes the question of whether to eat 'before or after' … Deciding 'before' might be more effective as an enticement, Wolf feeds her across the table from his fork, insisting she taste the chicken for its texture, firm to the bite, the flesh unravelling as it's rolled around her mouth by her ever-active tongue.

And then to the more sought-after pleasures of the night. At any time she might drown on the juices unleashed inside her body, she thinks. She feels the length of this stranger's torso as they sit side-by-side on the tight-fit lounge. He unlocks her folded arms, guiding her right hand to touch his knee, as he rests his elbow on her shoulder. As she sits and he stands, full-frontal, she pinches a hunk of tight flesh on the lower curve of his buttocks, and muzzles his flat belly, feeling the length of his hanging loose cock against her chest.

They move to lie on the bed, she still fully-clothed. He's had a shower already and wears a white fluffy bathrobe. He flops onto his back and pulls her hands gently to have her fall lightly onto his body, as he opens up the bathrobe to show off his tanned body. Releasing the tension in her arms, she nestles into his chest as she rubs her covered vulva against his naked cock.

She travels just a small distance to the border that sensuality shares with lust, and is lucky enough to return serene. Sensations of forced patience criss-cross his face as he shows her the strength in his arms to capture and keep her, then let her go free. This is the last chance tonight she'll have to walk away unfettered, she knows.

As she stands, he follows her and they kiss again. She is leaving, she says.

'Another kiss?' he cajoles.

'Only if it's a little one, a good one, a proper one.'

'I won't give those. If you want a kiss from me you must have it the way I give it.'

'Alright, but it's the last, it must be the very last,' she states, wavering between blank and emphatic expression in her voice. She now senses some danger.

He recedes in the kiss, trying to pull her forward to him. Her tongue pushes into the entrance to the gulf of his mouth, finding his teeth, and behind them, his tongue, strong and still.

He's receding further, she knows now, because of her edicts. Her understanding that 'he wants me to follow' is mixed with a fear she's losing her identity – and will perhaps lose a great deal more than that – if she goes any further. So she stalls, and pats his chest constantly with her left hand to comfort and confuse him a little, as she withdraws.

It's over. Cupid has already left in disgust at her faintheartedness.

'You married people are always in such a rush to get it over … thinking about how you have to put the cat out,' he snipes. The only tinge of bitterness he allows himself.

Striding down the long corridor, she laughs nervously, chattering to him about just going out for a minute to put the cat out the back, no through the front door, because otherwise he might pee on the sage in her back yard. It's her own home, her own yard, her own man she's thinking of. The wolf follows her, edgy.

'Don't you have a business card you could give me?' he asks.

'No.'

'Why not?'

'What's the point?' her voice rasps out, forcing the air from her lungs to sound out the words.

'Well, good luck in your life, if I don't see you again. I'd like to see you again though.'

Civil to the barren end – as they reach the elevator and she presses the button hard.

'Maybe in your next life?' he asks.

Her eyes agree with a light in his, in a final spark of hope that quickly turns to hurt. Was his question 'next life', or 'next flight', she wonders.

She doesn't have to watch the melancholy in his face for long. As she swivels her head towards the lift door, she imagines a pale mask in place of his features.

Later she thinks about the person behind the façade of love she'd encountered on the plane: a former doctor, now turned financier who'd been in the military, and loved a budgerigar called Mac that would perch on his shoulder, and initially loved a beautiful wife, but not by the end of their marriage. What parts of his story were true, she wondered?

This man had left a small thorn in her heart, not big enough to cause bleeding, she knew. She was spared since she hadn't inhaled a full draught of the heady perfume of intoxication of 'other' this time.

When she'd first spoken to him as they'd sat side-by-side on the flight, he'd seemed a typical young business executive. He'd been wearing a blue linen suit, but she couldn't remember having seen a tie. He'd projected an image of little constraint between mind and body, thought and action. She found later that without any need to add flourish to his Adam's apple, there was little lost pride when decoration was abandoned. Abandonné.

Later that night in another hotel room several kilometres away from the cautionary black vase, she dreams she is drowning in fluid love. She's filled with a pleasure that is water within and around her. She looks up to the daylight of sky and sees turbid air bubbles surging above her head, across her shoulders, tickling her underarms, stroking her body and tingling her toes. She is water and air in turbulence, a zephyr awash.

One week later she dreams she is in a room in Paris, looking out of a leadlight window made up of squares of tinted green glass, and on the window sill, ready to be drunk in through the senses, are two white roses with edges tinged in pink, standing in a clear glass vase. It is morning and he has left her a rose to show his love.

On waking she wonders if now is the right time to start a new life, cultivating pastel roses in place of geraniums.

# The Solace of Daughters

*Is it not a matter for laughter*
*to debate about past and future, unaware of the present?*
Sri Ramana Maharshi 'The Direct Way'

This week I've felt the sense of contentment I had as a young mother. It's in the air, in the sunny, early autumn days spent living in Sydney's beach suburbs. I used to watch my toddler's toes beside mine splashing in seashore puddles, I'd feel the pores of my upper back soak up the mild sunshine that haloed her outline, and hear parrots out-chattering her babble. We enjoyed each day in a code of loving. Drew from a deep well of trust.

I was telling my eldest daughter, now grown, about that time when I'd been simply happy, but she didn't want to hear … because that time was shattered for her as a girl. Her parents split; the peach cleaved in two. She must have thought I wanted it whole again; but I want it otherwise, while she seeks that first contentment still. So she must find it for herself in another form.

Now I understand there is only once for everything. And then there's something else.

In those early years, I would sing her a song my father had in turn sung for me. His trembling tenor voice exposing a gentleness and innocence that his roughened, dark-tanned, hirsute body could never completely hide, he would lift his head high, chin tilted, and embark on an age-old theme:

*One day I saw two lovers in a garden*
*A gentle boy and girl with golden hair.*
*At first I thought that I would ask their pardon*
*On second thoughts I watched the youthful pair.*
*The boy, all blushing, gave the girl a kiss*
*And tenderly he whispered this:*
*'I'll be your sweetheart*
*If you will be mine.*
*All my life*
*I'll be your valentine.*
*Bluebells we'll gather*
*Keep them and be true.*
*When I'm a man my plan*
*Will be to marry you.*

A second verse describes the narrator passing that garden again only to find a couple with silver hair living that once-golden vision. My mother, who's aged eighty-eight, reminded me of a few words from the first verse but had forgotten everything of the second. My father's no longer around to retouch her fading sepia image.

\*

World-travelled several times over and I find myself back in an old setting, just metres from where, so many years ago - when I was not much older than that golden haired girl - I suffered a shattering of childhood romance. Here tonight a second rendezvous is enacted under the landmark Coca-Cola sign at the top of The Cross – where everything but the neon blaze has now aged. At once my life is both 'the real thing' and a 'reality check': I'm fifty and we're all here to celebrate my eldest daughter's twenty-ninth birthday. In the very same building - can its geomancy be so strong? But renovations have turned the once-was coffee shop into trendy Japanese eating-houses: high-class 'XU' on one side; downmarket 'Ju-Ju's' on the other.

As we arrive I feel a warmth of welcome billow out from the crowd already there, and see my eldest daughter shining. But my youngest daughter is on edge. High-pitched and pacey, she feels the barbs of other young women's eyes in the group. The feeling is just as acute to her whether real or imagined, I observe. Her father, my second husband, feels at one remove. We take up our roles as if they're familiar yet ill-fitting overcoats. Mother, half-sister and step-father to the birthday girl.

Her father, my first husband, is on the other side of the globe, absent from his eldest daughter's birthday celebration, represented instead by his eldest son, now nineteen and studying a media course at a university where I teach. His girlfriend is in my class. He's a handsome young man, close to the age his father was when we first met, and like him, shy and innocent enough to blush. He tells me his father is hatching chickens in a home incubator to mark the end of a long European winter.

As I'd approached the party venue I'd realised that this was the place where I'd witnessed my first husband's betrayal. My strong ego, my self-esteem, the confidence I had in my beauty and the love he gave me – back then all were ripped open with just one look. As a cadet journalist bursting with ambitious pride, I strode into the coffee-shop to meet him and his art college friends, all at ease lounging around a table. This was his group and I the outsider. Squeezing in beside him, I saw a girl with a beautiful face sitting opposite us. Then I saw her plead with her eyes, her gaze fixed on his. I didn't see his face; I didn't need to; I couldn't bear to. Later I accused, and he denied. It made no difference to the truth I had recognised. A few years later when at the age of twenty-six I left him for another man, the girl moved in with him within a week or two. After all, he was the victim and I the guilty party. I had moved out and was even refusing to pay my share of the mortgage. So I signed the property over to him for a sum received on paper only. It was the least I could do after breaking asunder our happy family, with our daughter aged just four. To be free of betrayal forever, I'd hoped. His new marriage lasted just long enough to produce two children. What's in a look?

Tonight I feel benevolence towards all these troubled twenty-somethings, seething, circulating, with eyes alight. I'm careful to keep mine lidded these days: no passion, no pain.

This evening, after I saw that the setting was the same, I was also relieved to witness the progeny of our second choices – my youngest daughter and his eldest son –

helping each other across the dangerous ground which is the rivalry of these older predators, more knowing than the younger pair could imagine. Finding themselves wedded as outsiders.

He's a quiet boy and I see that he has calmed her. For her part, perhaps she gives him some excitement. They discover a deep well to draw on for the moment. I wonder whether he's thinking of his girlfriend, and I can only marvel at how sexual attraction is such a mystery. The uncontrollable force of life manifesting. All at once, yet stretched from birth to death.

It's as if I'm living Incan time, the present paralleled in past and future.

And my second husband expects to pay off our mortgage within the week. Now there's emotional security for you. A sturdy substitute for passion.

Miracle enough that my mother's blood flows through my daughters' veins recycled endlessly by the moon. Yet little consolation that each of us must navigate the rips and currents of lust in our blood alone before at last we're released from the supper table to go our separate ways.

# A glistening afternoon

*In their time, both past and future are only the present.*
Sri Ramana Maharshi 'The Direct Way'

Once upon a glistening afternoon … stillness prevails as the eucalypts surrounding my home soak in the sunshine. What I'm feeling – this calm – this glow – shall I call it love? Or even the sensation of God?

There have been afternoons on this scale of exquisite sensation before. How many more to come? I will breathe in, breathe out, my chest gently scooping up this joyful tranquility. I fold myself into these moments, which stretch beyond the peak of half past three, heading towards dusk.

Sobering visits during the morning, as I escaped the drudgery of manipulating clauses, juggling email cut and paste, and referencing in-text citations.

My grandmother aged ninety-one is sleeping in the chair that confines her in the lounge room of a nursing home. As I arrive she's not just lounging, but sleeping. Her arms crossed and tucked up on the lunch table; her head resting on the chair's high metal edge. She stirs and opens her mouth to receive a chunk of chocolate.

Further down the road a friend has cancer and her 'year to live' deadline in September creeps up to engulf her. We talk of politics and art and 'Who cares about human rights any more anyway, since this theme doesn't sell in a mass market?' She avoids the main issue: how to confront, at the same time as ignore, Death stalking her pleasures.

Words come tumbling from my mouth. I say that my grandmother has been keen 'to go' for a long time but no one arrives to take her. My friend's side-long glance takes in another message. A direct hit. I didn't mean to hurt but cannot take back the words that resonate now. What are friends for? We hug at the door.

A fast-paced turn about the park and I'm back at my writing desk, struggling to stay seated and overcome my growing aversion to the computer screen. What, more bad news? This time another close friend, the blow delivered by an unfamiliar email address. She's resigned from the school due to pressing health problems, an uncertain prognosis. It's not mentioned, but a recurring word, 'cancer', seeps into my thoughts. How to write comforting words that don't sound morbid or insincere? After all, it's not her funeral yet. She's strong; she'll fight it.

Immediately the phone calls begin to queue, responding to doubts raised by the cc'd message. Who'll take her place? Can we change tomorrow's meeting time? What will happen to her projects?

I walk away from the clamour, and a glistening afternoon envelops my mind. Stillness prevails as the eucalypts surrounding my home soak in the sunshine. One day, every day, while ever I live, I might savour nature's glory. The same sensation: felt in childhood, middle age, old age. All is as one within a peaceful mind. All ages in one moment.

So soon it's after 4 o'clock. The sun leaves me alone to stare westward, as darkness begins to fall deep down my spine.

A chill settles in as I rise to rejoin the working world.

# Sydney Syd

Syd was nudging eighty when he met Annie. She'd looked a bit helpless, asking the bus driver to tell her which stop to get off. She was quite practised at the helpless act, of course, but he wasn't to know that. Annie was new in town. He'd looked over all the old girls thereabouts. She cut quite a figure, and wouldn't have been easily overlooked.

He'd tapped her on the shoulder and told her that her stop was his too, so they could get off together.

Syd had lost his wife the year before from Parkinson's. He'd been spared the last dismal months when a patient cannot feed herself, cannot walk, cannot recognize loved ones. His wife had gone into hospital for an operation and never came out again. Still, he'd paid his dues for a couple of years before she died – he did all the cooking and washing, even bathing her and helping her on the toilet and to dress.

Annie had lost her husband from Parkinson's too. It didn't take her long to recognize the same symptoms in Syd. Don't get too involved, her family warned her. She needed company and admiration, he always paid when they went out and he doted on her. How could she not get involved?

Syd was a real gentleman, her daughters and sons agreed with her. He'd been the last of thirteen children and was given a special name after the city in which he was conceived and born.

Lucky thirteen. A lucky boy, he loved his mother, and helped her by getting a job as soon as he was old enough.

It wasn't all easy street though, being born in the teens of the nineteen hundreds. He'd had a hard life, helping his mother look after the children of his older sisters.

But he'd learnt early how to acquit himself on the dance floor. And he'd found a reliable job on the railways and stayed with it, working his way up into management.

He took Annie dancing up at the Labor Club. He wasn't a Labor man himself, voting informal most of his life. But he soon learnt to keep any political opinions to himself when Annie was around. In turn she learnt not to ask him what he thought about current affairs – her opinions were strong enough for two in any case.

Syd loved women and children - it was evident from his conversation.

'Old women' was not in his vocabulary – they were all girls, and those with grey hair were 'blondes'.

And he was very fond of Annie's granddaughter, Justine. She was just eight yet had a wit almost as dry as his. He paid her for it in chocolate. He had one daughter who was in her fifties. That would have made him in his late twenties when she was born. She had a son and daughter. It was a neat little family group.

A few days before he died he'd told his daughter that she should have had brothers and sisters.

'It's too late now, Pop,' she'd remarked, trying to be comforting.

It was all too late, and he had regrets. He told Annie about them.

When the first child was about a year old his wife had become pregnant again, and gone off with her sister and had an abortion without telling him. His wife hadn't said a word but her sister had kindly told him. She'd said it was a boy. Very sisterly, thought Annie.

He was so hurt he 'made sure his seed never passed that way again'. So they'd never had any more children.

'It was your own fault,' Annie told him.

'I couldn't ever forgive her,' his dry throat scratched out.

Imagine the long cold years of mutual bondage. Bitter chill lovemaking. Cool conversations at table afterwards. He'd stayed faithful to his wife through those barren years, stretching into their old age and companionship.

They went dancing a lot. Annie had seen a photo of him in his younger days in a tuxedo, with his wife in a glittering ball dress by his side. And again dressed to the nines at his daughter's wedding.

After his wife died he still went dancing a lot.

Then Annie came along and she loved to dance – not only with him unfortunately. Still she was loyal enough in her way. She just wanted to kick up her heels a bit.

One spring morning they'd sailed away on a pacific cruise together, sharing a cabin. Syd never dreamt he could be so happy. No one in the family asked who slept in the top bunk.

Back home he would bring Annie fruit from the markets and cakes from the corner bakery. But never flowers. 'I'm not the flowers type,' he'd explain. Annie knew that he'd had too many years of penny-pinching to be able to lash out on flowers. Besides, he said, there were only two sorts that were worth looking at, roses and carnations, and they were always the most expensive at the local fruit store. When he and Annie went out to the pictures, or lunch, he would use his free gold bus pass. Annie, who preferred to go by taxi, told him one day as she waited with him in the wind at a bus stop that he had 'a bus mentality'. It was her not-so-subtle way of saying he was mean with his money.

She'd let him stay over one night a week, but never more than that. She'd waited sixty years for her freedom.

He had his freedom too, of course. Off to the races every Saturday for a flutter. He reckoned he came out ahead by the end of the year. He was a 'philosophe'. Lacking the wild, excitable nature of most punters, he concentrated on short odds.

When his Parkinson's advanced so that he had to go to a nursing home, Annie thought she might shake him off a bit. She went to the races herself for a sunny midweek meeting. There she met a nice elderly fellow, and saw him again on the Saturday. It was only on the second occasion that she caught his name: 'Syd, short for Sydney,' he boasted. That turned her blood cold. Her other Syd's surname was Vines and she felt in his grip indeed.

So Annie took to visiting her old, faithful Syd in his nursing home. She laid down the law in most things. And didn't she ever have a temper? Her faithful old Syd couldn't stand it when she'd put on a turn. 'Whatever you like,' he'd say.

'I could make her happy if only she'd let me,' he'd tell Annie's daughter, imploring her to speak in his favor.

'No you can't, so don't worry about it, Syd,' the daughter told him. She didn't want to elaborate about her own father being the one to make her mother happy, and now he was gone forever, but if he'd pressed a bit harder she would have thrown it at him. He knew when to keep quiet.

The daughter changed her mind one evening when she walked into her mother's lounge room and there sat her father on the lounge, as usual, just like in their old house.

She stared at him full in the face. Her father was dead – gone two years – yet there he was. She stared, her eyes straining, and beyond a floating misty space before her eyes Syd's features settled into the accustomed lines. She sat down abruptly.

Still she couldn't bring herself to hug him hard, to hug him whole, like she had her Dad. She was polite and gentle but always held back a bit.

The strange thing was that her own husband was beginning to remind her of her father. She would glance at his dark hair at an angle three quarters to the back, and start. He was developing a jowl like her father used to have. And when their daughter jumped up onto his lap and he cradled her in to his body, just watching she felt the physical warmth of it.

Funny, because Annie said Syd reminded her of her own father, gentle and quiet.

There were so many fathers in the world, all in the process of ageing from arrogant tyrant, protective of dependents, to helpless dependent in need of protection. If you lived long enough you'd see it in every man.

One summer's day when Syd was still able to get out and about, he returned to his flat and hunted about for treasure. He'd buried it in wall cavities over the years, in a space behind the bed and another behind the wardrobe. He came up with 'ten thou' - enough for the moment.

The money was pushed into Annie's hand on her next visit as he told her bitterly about his daughter being mean and investing his life's savings so he wouldn't spend it. He wanted Annie to have what he could get his hands on.

'I'll keep seven for you,' Annie told him. 'If you ever need it just let me know.' But it wasn't long before it burnt her fingers. She sent him postcards from Dublin and the Aegean.

Syd reckoned Annie would find herself a millionaire over there and he counted the days until she was home again. While she was gone he worried how he could come by more of his buried treasure so she would continue to visit him. 'Otherwise I think it'll be over between us,' he sombrely informed Annie's daughter.

One autumn day, his granddaughter went to visit him and told him that she had come across some money while cleaning out his flat so that it could be let.

'Don't tell me how much it was, nor anyone else,' he said. 'Just hold onto it.'

Then one bright, crisp winter's day, Syd went to sleep in the sunshine while sitting in his usual spot outside the nursing home, with his hat on to shade his face.

When his daughter came to visit, she couldn't wake him. She shook him again and again and there was not a movement in any part of his body that she could see.

She rushed inside to see the matron who came out and shook him hard. Nothing. Another nurse was called, a wheelchair brought, and he was wheeled into his room.

He woke on his bed, not knowing how he got there, or why so many faces were peering at him.

Syd was put into his pyjamas and kept in bed to rest, like a naughty child.

He told Annie he would have 'preferred that they let me die in peace'.

On Annie's next visit, accompanied by her daughter, Syd cried out as they arrived: 'I prayed to God he'd take me away from this pain last night'.

'Well, I prayed that you wouldn't die because I'm just not up to it'. Annie had spent a sleepless night too, after visitng her late husband's grave.

'About half past two in the morning,' they agreed, both with tears in their eyes.

When Annie's daughter apologised for not having visited him in a long time, he said he wished she hadn't seen him in this state.

'Don't be silly,' she interrupted. 'Of course I want to see you – it doesn't matter what you look like. I'll come again in a few weeks.'

Later she repeated that she hadn't seen him in a while, wanting to make amends for neglecting him, and he took the opportunity to make up for the rebuff he'd given her a few minutes earlier.

'And I'm very pleased you came to see me today,' he said, quietly leaning forward, always the gentleman.

Annie said he was worried about his gold filling missing from his front tooth. Where had it gone? He was so deathly white and cold, Annie's daughter hadn't noticed his teeth at all at first.

She had asked him for a smile, though, and he'd looked so pained and ill at ease. But he'd given it, the stubble creasing as his lips were pulled back over his teeth. Just like a small boy, trying to be good, or a lean, young dog learning how to cringe.

Months before, he'd given up reading the form, and wasn't allowed to walk any further than the corner of the street. These days he couldn't even walk a few steps. It took three people to hoist him out of his chair and onto the bed, only to repeat the movement in reverse a few minutes later when he looked quite uncomfortable and wasn't able to sit up straight without a backrest.

He'd tried to walk so many times but kept falling. He wouldn't give up – too much of the sense of freedom in his blood from years of jumping on and off trains and, later, buses, on his excursions all over the city.

Luckily, living in the nursing home, he hadn't got to the stage where they tie you down. Lucky? Because if it wasn't for the falls which bruised and bashed his forehead, Syd wouldn't have had the blood clot which caused the stroke.

Otherwise he might still be there – eating spoon-fed food he gagged on called steak and kidney, which used to be his favorite and now tasted like slush; given enemas; rubbed with lukewarm washers as a substitute for bathing; his body of white skin over whiter bones, flesh depleted, perched in one awkward position after another until even the sheepskins on the mattress couldn't prevent the bedsores spreading down his legs and the gangrene spreading up. Until a strong head and pumping heart was all that was left as the memorial of a stubborn, unforgiving but gentle man.

You might think a man couldn't die of boredom, but he could certainly die from lack of stimulation by carers. Yet Syd's wit lasted until the end.

'So what's your news, Syd? What's been happening?' Annie asked.

'No news is good news' – they chimed in unison.

'It's a fallacy,' he complained.

'No, I do have good news,' Annie fairly crowed. 'My son is on his feet again financially. He's set up a company and the money is flowing in. Reckons he'll make a million by the time he's fifty and will stash it away to hide it from the taxman. Now there's good news, Syd.'

With a wealthy son, what woman needs a father figure, he must have thought?

On Annie's next visit, Syd talked about the pain in his head and Annie told him, again, not to die yet because she wasn't strong enough to cope. He told her she was a funny one. Bitter humour. She never saw him again.

\*

Annie's neighbour, whose gruffness belied a sensitive nature, gave Annie two red carnations, grown in her garden and picked with the morning dew on them, to place on Syd's coffin. No store-bought blooms to disturb Syd's well-earned rest.

# A Nonconformist Spirit Guide

Travel guides while on holiday? Not a bit of it. What can be more satisfying than to find your own trail of personal interest and follow it?

I'd gone to the National Portrait Gallery in London and there seen a picture of Virginia Woolf. The caption included some information about the home in Gordon Square of her friend, Lytton Strachey, writer, bohemian, member of the Bloomsbury set. You'd not find this fact easily on Google maps, nor in most travel guides. So the next day, off I set to find Gordon Square.

Number 51 was the street number cited on the portrait's caption – a few doors along from Number 46, home of the late famous economist John Maynard Keynes, who'd lived there from 1916-1946, the year of his death. Before he moved there Virginia's sister, Vanessa Bell, the artist, and her husband, Clive, had lived together in the house, even while they were each having affairs. And even earlier, the house had been the home of the four siblings, Vanessa, Thoby, Virginia and Adrian after their father, Sir Leslie Stephen, the first editor of the Dictionary of National Biography, died in 1904. His offspring all lived in Number 46 until 1907. It's where the 'Thursday evenings' of recitals, readings and animated talk had given birth to the legend and name, the Bloomsbury set, comprising mainly Thoby's friends: Leonard Woolf, a publisher who would marry Virginia; Lytton Strachey, a noted biographer of two English queens who had a complicated cross-gender love life; Clive Bell, who would marry Vanessa; David Garnett [let me come back to David Garnett, a writer, publisher and bookshop owner who had an even more complicated love life]; Duncan Grant, an artist who had an affair with Virginia's brother Adrian before Adrian's later fruitful marriage and his interest in early Freudian psychology; John Maynard Keynes, a titan of twentieth century economics; and Roger Fry, an artist and critic who in 1910 would ascribe the title Post-Impressionism to French painting of that period.

But I didn't know all this detail at the time. There I was, an innocent abroad, delighted that I'd come upon this literary treasure in Gordon Square. I viewed a plaque on the front wall of Number 46 which gave the years of Keynes' residency, then moved along the street seeking Number 51. No plaque at the entrance. When I ventured up the few steps to the door and looked at the list of tenants' buzzers there was no mention there either of Virginia ever having been associated with the house.

Please forgive my familiar use of her Christian name only, but I half felt she was leading me on, because right then a fellow bounced up the steps, unlocked the door with his key, walked through and held the door open for me. Into the inner sanctum I stepped, and his large frame bounced a few more times as he sped up a flight of stairs to the first floor. Alone, standing stockstill on the ground floor, suddenly I felt small. I peeped through a half-open door into a room set with chairs lined up as if for a talk. By or about a posthumous writer, I wondered? But I didn't enter the room. A couple of other doors were locked. What to do? I decided it would be unsettling if I went upstairs and announced myself to the occupants, having bypassed the security system. I'd rather not have had to introduce myself as an intruder.

So I walked outside again and took note of some of the tenants' business names listed on the security buzzer.

Oh well, 'Level 1 Occupational Health and Safety', that's as good a place as any to start, I thought. It would turn out to be a hand full of aces.

'Yes?' the buzzer asked me politely.

'Oh, hello. I'm from Australia ... and my name is Crystal Williams. I'm an independent researcher ...' So what? Big deal, I think.

'... and I've read that Virginia Woolf ... ['Give her full title,' I decide] ... the novelist and early feminist, Virginia Woolf, lived here once. I'm wondering if you know anything about that.'

'Well, we're not officially on a literary trail or anything; this is a section of University College London, you know.'

'Oh, I'm sorry. I didn't know.'

'Perhaps you'd best come upstairs ...' The buzzer's voice had softened.

The buzzer went zzzz and the door went click, and in I burst. Up the stairs and there was a smiling fellow welcoming me into his office. Mr Average Clerical, with a propensity for setting down and implementing rules to protect workers. A genial accommodating fellow with a secret admiration for the antics on and off the page of the Bloomsbury group.

'This was actually the home of Lytton Strachey, and if you just walk through here ...'

At this point several men and women sitting behind computer screens and standing behind low shelves smile and nod in encouragement.

'... I can take you into the room next door, right here,' he says, opening another door.

The walls and doors are painted white, I note, as we move into an empty room with a fireplace and a white painted mantel piece, with windows facing bare plane trees surrounding Gordon Square.

'Oh, this is so kind of you.'

'Yes, not many people know about it, but this was Lytton's mother's home – and I've done a bit of research, and written a brief description which I've placed here on the wall, in honour, in memory ...' he says as he indicates for me to read the dedication.

I fumble about in my bag for my glasses and see on the wall beside the dedication a photograph of Lytton's mother taken from Michael Holroyd's 1971 biography of the great biographer himself.

'And here she is sitting, warming herself by this fireplace.' Mr Clerk's voice is positively tender.

I can almost feel heat coming off the fire-setting place of the absent grate, even in the midst of the room's lukewarm air conditioning. In fact I'm standing exactly where Mrs Lytton is sitting. Our parallel universes have merged. A white-haired dame, I bet she knew a thing or two in her time. This really is the 'innermost inner sanctum'.

And here is my escort pulling back the original locks at the top and bottom of the glass-and-timber doors. His arm gestures for me to step onto the narrow balcony. I stand under the wintry plane trees which, leafless, offer me a clear view of the lawns and greenery so neatly trimmed in Gordon Square below.

I actually lean on the balcony railing, swing my hips this way and that, imagining being part of a conversation between Virginia and her sister, Vanessa, who'd lived in the office I'd just walked through, I'm told.

At some point I become self-conscious. How long is polite, I wonder, to indulge in a reverie of sisterhood and letters. The kind fellow hasn't stepped outside with me, so it must be time to come in. Yes, the air is slightly chilly.

'But I'd like to show you the family crest, if I may – and if you have the time. It should only take a few minutes. Just up these stairs.'

And we're rising up the original staircase, and towards the rear of the building, past a 1960s renovated kitchen, and then into view comes the small backyard and a row of weathered slate and metal roofs on the terraces behind.

A stained glass window in the back room displays what I'm informed is the Lytton family crest. I wouldn't know one crest from another but this fine fellow has checked it out. I can only feel grateful that he's nominated himself as curator of this prized stained glass artefact.

Thanking him profusely for the special impromptu viewing, I tumble out of the house, feeling blessed by lucky stars and a boldness in intruding into the University's workaday world for the sake of my own pleasure.

I wander through the Square's garden and pick a red rose, imagining Virginia and Vanessa's earlier snitching, then begin to walk a rectangular circuit of the park via the footpath, until I stop, a seeming vision before my eyes.

'Dr Williams' Philosophical Library.' Established originally in 1729 in Cripplegate and moved to Gordon Square in 1890.

Dr Williams? But that's me! Another parallel universe soft collision. I've just left behind in Australia a poetry and philosophy library, a 'reading retreat', I'd established the previous year.

Here in Gordon Square the library's double doors are locked so I proceed to announce myself to another buzzer security system as an independent researcher from Australia, and I am cordially invited upstairs amidst the arcane collection.

What to touch, what to find, among these hundreds of books stacked high to the ceiling?

Fortunately there's a sale of some contemporary texts, Indian philosophy no less, my primary interest of late. I buy a bundle of books at a pound a copy, and finding I can't carry them all as well as hold onto my red rose, I offer the rose to a young woman behind the desk. She's pleased.

So am I. Packing up these precious texts of ancient knowledge ever so carefully, I cart them through several European countries before landing back home.

*

So the story ends there, you think?

No. This year, a good five years later, I'm back in London with my social economist partner, and I swear I'll take him on the mini-Woolf tour. We view Number 46, home to his youthful people's hero, John Maynard Keynes. I'm excited as we move along the street. We're standing before the row of houses: Now which is it, what number was that, I wonder? Yes, it must be this one, Number 51.

There's the buzzer. There's the Occupational Health and Safety label. There's the disembodied voice in response to my buzzing. I begin my routine.

'Hello, I'm an Australian ...'

'Yes, you'd better come up.'

At the top of the stairs there's a fellow grinning, and I feel a little embarrassed. Is it him? I've forgotten his face. But he knows mine, and quickly resumes his literary guide routine, after the introduction of my partner.

The photo, the fireplace, the balcony – and this time it's summer so the plane trees have their broad sheltering leaves on display for us, blocking the view of the park. Then up the stairs to see the Lytton family crest.

Mr Guide tells me his Unit will be moving to new premises within a few months, so he doesn't know what will become of the office, the fireplace, the original stairs or the crest.

We offer prayers that they will be valued enough by the new occupants to remain in situ.

Next, down to the park, and I see a spectacular red rose which I must have.

'Come and see the Philosophical Library,' I call to my partner and, pronto, there we are before the ancient timber double doors, pressing the buzzer, once again being invited up.

Again there's a book sale, and would you believe, this time there are books that suit my current disposition? A heavy two-volume set of Boswell's Life of Johnson, Keats' correspondence and The Life of Saint Teresa among them. They'll do just fine for my memoir classes! And not an Indian philosophical book in sight this time. How uncanny!

My partner buys me a Dr Williams' Philosophical Library bag and I'm well on my way with the heavy load slung over my shoulder. But wait, I can't carry all these books as well as hold onto my rose, so I'll just give ....

Ping. A little light goes on in my memory bank as I see myself repeating the gesture. The girl is charmed, accepting the gift. I wonder how many times Virginia may have absent-mindedly gone through the same routine.

And later, once I'm back at my daughter's home in Queensway, I check some documents that I brought with me from Australia to track down the area of London where my great great great grandmother lived before she came out to the colony on a sailing ship. I find that it's Islington – and you'll never guess which library holds many of the records of 19th century and earlier Nonconformists (that is, anyone who held non-Church of England religious beliefs, such as Baptists, Congregationalists, Recusants, Catholics, Quakers, Jews).

Yes, Dr Williams' Philosophical Library, which was first located in Islington, or Cripplegate as it was known in the early 1800s. It's the area where my forebear, Maria Rivers lived, close by a church now renovated to its original condition, known for a golden dragon on its steeple.

Nonconformist, I hear your mind questioning? Who could have been more non-conformist than William Blake, renowned for his attacks on conventional religion? A contemporary of my great great great grandmother, Blake died in 1827, possibly the year she came to Australia, and he's buried in a Quaker Nonconformist burial ground about half a mile from the church with the dragon steeple. (Where, incidentally, the gardener who opened the gate for me told me he'd spent a few years living in the same beach suburb of Sydney as I lived.) Or who more non-conformist than Virginia's mother, who'd been a model for the Pre-Raphaelite painters, a movement begun in the 1850s? Or Virginia herself, who dressed in clothes to mimic an Abyssinian man, complete with false beard, and, along with others from the Bloomsbury group, inspected the ship HMS Dreadnought in 1910, pretending to be one of a delegation of Abyssinian royals, thereby embarrassing the Royal Navy and government of the day and making a public point about pacifism.

So, let's return to the story of David Garnett, a Bloomsbury writer whom I promised you had 'a complicated love life' ... no less so than Vanessa Bell (Virginia's sister). Garnett was bisexual and at one time had an affair with another Bloomsburyite, Duncan Grant, also bisexual. Duncan went on to produce a child with Vanessa Bell. After attending the birth of this daughter of his two close friends, Garnett wrote to another friend, 'I think of marrying it. When she is 20, I shall be 46 – will it be scandalous?' And yes, when the baby Angelica grew into her early twenties, she and Garnett married – but I don't know whether this marriage was more a matter of non-conforming within the Church of England or non-conforming outside of it.

Non-conformist behaviour enough, wouldn't you say? Wild lives extending back two centuries. And all discovered because I would not conform to an official travel guide, but rather, ventured off the beaten track between the National Portrait Gallery and Number 51 Gordon Square – led dreamily along perhaps by the hand of our Virginia.

# Turning Fifty

My youngest daughter came home to me.

At the age of 18, Layla had gone to Mexico for a year and her father and I had visited her after six months. But there was no word from her then about whether she'd return to Australia at the end of the year.

*Don't push her. Let her be,* I whispered to myself. *Maybe she'll tire of the place.*

She was living poorly, teaching English and travelling with a girlfriend from uni; she had a boyfriend in a small regional town in the mountains. 'Sippy sippy', the locals called the light rain which was a common weather pattern.

I did want her to come home to complete her degree in Sydney. I may have asked tangentially what her plans were. She was strong, independent, full of confidence despite her poor material life. Perhaps I didn't ask, after all. Better not to seem to be exerting any influence on her life's fortune.

My birthday falls at the end of January. Christmas came and went and we'd phoned and sent gifts. No word about her New Year's resolutions. I was pining.

By the end of the month, plans were afoot for my 50th birthday celebration, with my eldest daughter and my partner looking through my old contact books for the phone numbers of friends old and new.

Is she coming home, my older daughter, Talia, wanted to know.

No idea.

In fact, Talia had been secreting Layla away at her place for a whole week.

Until the morning of my birthday, as I'm ironing, there's an exclamation and I look up to see Layla standing in our lounge room. And then look down. I'm stunned. An apparition?

I take a second look, a longer look this time. I measure out the pleasure as I speed toward this image of great beauty before my eyes – created from my own flesh and blood.

No words can convey ...

# Travelling with Ganesh

He first caught my attention inside a temple cafe in Mumbai on that academic-confer-ence-and-research trip to India one winter early in the century. That's not quite true, as I, an Australian woman of indeterminate age and looks, had had intimate contact with him a couple of years before, while I was locked in an embrace with my lover. Not that I mean I looked down at my lover's penis and thought of Ganesh's trunk. No, it's not as obvious as that. Nothing like it. I mean he caught my whole attention, my whole being. In one breath I became Ganesh. I was Ganesh – he was me. Just like in a dream when fear takes you over completely, or ecstasy, and you wake trembling, remembering, realising that you aren't in that state of sensation any more, or like an overpowering sexual orgasm of a completely different order than its mere recollection.

But this wasn't dreaming or orgasm. This was Ganesh – the state, condition, flavour and essence of Ganesh. His ponderous being was every cell of my body. His physique overwhelmed my mind, stilled it, with a force so strong that I had no thoughts at all - I at-tended only to (the) being Ganesh. It wasn't as if I saw, smelt, heard or tasted him, or even touched the tail and mistook it for the whole – he seized my being so completely there was no difference between his flesh and mine. And I say 'he'. What else shall I call him? He was too sensuous to be called 'it'. There was nothing inert or neutered about him. He was a presence; physicality itself. Yet I didn't feel that I'd changed gender, had suddenly become masculine. I was simply all limbs and trunk and sensation - warm and tingling through and through. As Ganesh took me over, I enveloped my lover. Later we reached orgasm – that was much the same for me as usual. Ganesh didn't have time to hang about for that.

So when he caught my attention again outside a temple cafe in Mumbai I wasn't at all surprised. Not that I was taken over body and soul like that first time. This was fleeting, a mere cerebral flash, a wink and a nod from a doorway across a lane. I'd just been to meet a sage who gave me the same advice I'd heard last year, the only advice one needs in life, 'Enlightenment or faith is established once, and only when, you surrender to the grace of God. So simply accept, and then you can get on with living the experience of life.'

At the guru's satsang I'd met an Israeli man whose name was taken from the Koran and meant 'serious', and an Australian woman who also liked elephants. Then there was an Englishman who became more agitated the more dope he smoked, thinking he was getting calmer (or 'karma', perhaps) and who believed in this guru's theme of fate; and finally, a German who guided us to the temple cafe. They all wanted a meal and I went along with them to see the temple, waited while they ate and then forgot all about entering that sacred place because we played a game instead. It was a long psychology game because we each had to think of our favourite ... etc., and give three reasons why, and the dope-smoker worried constantly about which word he wanted to use to best describe what he meant.

'You think too much. Just feel,' I told him.

Then I turned my attention to the most energetic member of our ad hoc group.

'This is a game, and according to the raison d'être of games, it's just for fun and to pass the time. Isn't that right?' I enquired of Mr Serious, who had a strong nose and receding hairline, despite his youth. He also had a buzz coming off him. Something would happen when he looked at your eyes, or was it your forehead? A blank space. A dark patch, a glitch in transmission. He had deep, dense eyes.

He laughed to show his sensuous personality. His favourite animal was a lion or tiger. We found out later that your favourite animal represented your sexual partner. The Englishman's was a cat, since it was aloof or distant, he couldn't decide which.

'Or is it you who's distant?' I asked.

Herr Templeman's favourite animal was a panther and I and the other woman chose elephants, so we were restricted in our choices for some reason. Clannishness, born of being on the road, maybe. I chose an elephant for its characteristics of calm, sensibility (for elephants mourn the deaths of their own kind when they come upon a gravesite) and physicality. Just the same as for Ganesh, I explained.

Mr Serious laughed heartily and I thought, 'This man loves sex'.

I stood up so I could view him more directly without craning my neck to see past the other elephant-loving girl. And then Ganesh caught my eye. He was sitting above a doorway across the lane, compact and self-contained, shooting a twinkling glance in my direction, so that we bonded for an instant.

'And here's Ganesh watching over us all the while,' I announced, as if trumpeting this synchronicity.

It was obvious that none of Ganesh's physicality was lost on Mr Serious. As she talked, the girl who was fond of elephants found reasons to touch his lower arm, his upper arm, his shoulder, his back. She'd only just landed in India the night before and the initial confusion of the sub-continent was disorienting her, causing over-stimulation of the senses.

After our word game we went to the Hanging Gardens, which were not hanging at all, but bolt upright, primmed and trimmed and hedged, a leftover from the Raj, with topiary curiosities from the far-flung corners of the Empire on display: emu following kangaroo; rhinoceros leading camel.

The Englishman asked directions of someone with little knowledge of the terrain so we were left to amble about in search of the Parsee corpses' tower until we were stopped at a roadblock by hijras, known as eunuchs or transvestites to Westerners. The Englishman played the fool, acting up a scene of being terrorised and running off, with squeals of mock alarm that he might be ravaged. But Mr Serious stood his ground and smiled enigmatically while one young fellow, sareed in vibrant yellow, wove his body about, snake-like, before him.

'Give me money,' the painted 'boy' grinned. 'I want money,' he chanted again.

'No money,' Mr Serious grinned back.

The boy grabbed my wrist and I felt a masculine iron grip beneath the folds of sari before I flung it off. Mr Serious seemed delighted as the boy placed his right hand, thumb to thumb, finger to finger against his own. The boy's nails were broad and very long, manicured to induce curling, with the remains of bright pink polish a sign of some previous enticement. The air was electric.

'Give me money.'

'No money.'

'Give me money.'

'No money.'

The chant died down as we turned away and strolled deliberately back to the Gardens' entrance.

Then the German went off about his business affairs while the elephant-fondling girl and the Englishman came along with me in a taxi on their way to the caves of Elephanta Island, home to a sacred lingam or phallic symbol. She was surprised to find herself stranded with the indecisive fellow when Mr Serious declined the expedition, claiming he had more to attend to in that decadent garden. No doubt he was searching for a delightful game to while away time, which hangs so heavy on sultry tropical afternoons. I too soon peeled away from the pair and found my own entertainment.

Early on in my trip I'd seen an article about outrage over disrespect shown to Ganesh at a Sleaze Ball in Sydney by homosexuals who'd used his image as their vanguard. This was a warning to me. I'd found Ganesh had a great sense of fun, magnanimous in the extreme, but only if you paid him the respect he was due. He was, after all, Shiva's son and carried this familial power. Where Shiva was both all-corporeal and non-corporeal simultaneously, Ganesh was manifest to those who recognised him. Or was it, whom he recognised? Shiva was hard to get your mind around, but Ganesh was just a lovable boy until and unless you failed to recognise the immense and sacred power within that shape. The power to grow, to rise, to intensify, to exalt. In an instant, innocent calm could turn to massive fury.

I'd also read an article about a girl attacked in a field by an elephant which took offence at something about her. And another story about an elephant which escaped from a Thai zoo because a visitor had teased it with food, and it ran wildly in the streets until sedated by a dart gun. But the family of elephants I'd seen in a national park, the party of four which allowed our bus to pass through their territory, flopping and curving their trunks about, were domesticity and docility itself. Our gracious hosts. Passengers were transfixed and an expiration of admiration, a murmur of love, resonated through the bus. Some chord deep within us was struck at the sight of our fellow ancient inhabitants of this planet. Elephants at peace with the world, undisturbed, grazing and tending their young – a scene of harmony outside of time.

My elephant travel snapshots continued, pointing the way to what I hoped would prove a satisfying culmination.

While sightseeing in Pondicherry, three times I bumped into two Englishwomen, so it was evident we were meant to talk. I told them about my bus trip cross-country in the middle of the night, boarding a bus for one town, Trichur, and discovering the destination was a town with a similar name in another state, Trichi, short for Trichupalli or Trichinopoly, also known as Tiruchchirappalli – citing the confusion as an example of cross-cultural linguistic bastardry, left over from English attempts at codification, that the locals were at ease with but which promptly tripped me up. I described how I was terrified when I got off the bus at three o'clock in the morning to find myself alone in a square, accosted by a motley group of auto rickshaw drivers and down-and-outs.

'I guess it was all about confronting my fears and accepting my lot. But I was very sorry I missed the first town because you can be blessed by an elephant there,' I explained.

'Oh you can be blessed in Trichupalli too. But I hear typhoid has broken out so I'm too nervous to go there.'

'I think anyone's blessed if they don't have typhoid,' I said. 'I haven't been blessed by an elephant but at least I'm still alive.'

I decide to stay put and avoid midnight buses. We of English stock know our good fortune, standing by a waterfront promenade in an exotic country, surrounded by the poor and maimed, beneficiaries of our largesse, or at least our small change. No further dialogue is needed to reinforce my humility and a sense that Ganesh, the travellers' guide, has me in hand.

That evening I call into a tourist information booth to ask about daytime bus services and find I'm also asking what temples are to be found there. Temples to the elephant god as well as to Shakti, Shiva's female energy force, are high on the list.

Next morning off I set to find Ganesh in his southern sub-continent Vinayaga form. But I discover Ganesh not only as Vinayaga - he lines the walls of the temple right up to the ceiling in one incarnation after another, from Chinese, Burmese, Thai, Lao, Malaysian and Indonesian guises, right through the Asian and South-East Asian network of related theologies. Sometimes his belly is full, sometimes he's more austere, but his trunk is always curled across a substantial corpus.

The climax comes when I meet the young royal in residence himself, snorting to clear the mucous from his tantalising trunk. I'm dazzled by his soft glance through dark lashes, as his pastel iris shyly penetrates my eyesight. His trunk's pale pink inside-flesh, tender and moist, takes from my hand the tufts of grass I offer. Gently.

And then the blessing.

'Step closer,' I'm instructed by the mahout. I step in and lean forward, my right hand out in front so I can avoid the complete trust you need to show when offering up the crown of your head to an over-sized, wrinkled, brown benefactor. The elephant caresses and blows on the back of my hand and I feel relief and pleasure. But it's not the full trust which carries with it a full blessing. I must surrender my all and offer my bowed head rather than my hand to receive a great gift.

'Step in closer,' the elephant's companion tells me as he lightly taps the slow-swinging trunk. I bow in submission to the kindness, and a blowing of breath, a cupping of touch, a ruffling of hair sends my senses soaring, my attention fully focussed on the pinnacle of my skull, the crown chakra. By the grace of Ganesh, what good fortune can come into my life? Later that afternoon I discover that a vaginal infection I've been suffering for days has disappeared.

Next on my Ganesh-guided trip I attend a post-colonial and millennial cultural theory conference in the north of the country. A woman lecturer gives a paper on homoerotica and violent penetration, oblivious of the grotesque symbolism of her ring-pierced lower lip which has been causing a shocking sensation within the traditional body-piercing culture of Rajasthan. The locals gape and guffaw, demanding to know why she's had her lip pierced and whether it hurts. They in turn are unaware of the source of their compulsion to pierce stretched earlobes and nostrils.

On the same conference panel as Ms Pierce, a male American Sikh scholar, long dark tresses tucked up under his turban, gives a paper titled, 'The Post-Secular Nose: Religiopus Differentials and the Territories of the Body'. I notice the interest of the two speakers in one another; they chat briefly at the end of the session. And once during her paper when she uses the word 'fuck' his eyes spark with mine. One click and then away. Later, several glances. His paper is erudite, clever, amusing. But for all that, I feel a little disinterested. I can sense the air from Ganesh's protuberance breezing about my locks, ruffling and snuffling. So much hot air. All talk, no action. I'm older and wiser than this young scholar, I think. What he needs is a good nudge. Dangling donger derring-do, as it were.

The following morning we three attend a garden session, wearing our sunglasses as protection from direct gazes. I can see them both, but a large Bo tree prevents them from seeing each other. She leaves after the first paper and as Ganesh removes all obstacles and the chairs are rearranged, the Sikh and I find ourselves sitting side by side. I have a clear view of his profile and, when he removes his sunglasses, his curled lashes.

'I'm older and wiser,' I remind myself. Now for the nudge, a potent proboscial push.

'Has anybody ever told you that you have a fine nose?' I ask, lowering my sunglasses to emphasise the point.

'Thank you.' He gives the same sensuous laugh as Mr Serious.

A younger, milder woman would have stopped point blank.

'So don't just think about it, or talk about it. Use it.'

He laughs again, obviously shocked and uncertain how to reply. But he bounces back and asks questions of the next speaker, and does not move away from me at the first opportunity. I know I am leaving immediately after lunch, but he does not know this and talks on to a friend about Communism in Kolkata and family pressures to marry. The lunch plates begin to be cleared away and I go to collect my luggage. As my taxi drives off I catch a glimpse of Mr Nose Singh and Ms Body Pierce bridging a cultural abyss in the shade of the Bo's branches. What is this if not the clearest manifestation of Mr Singh's direct link with Ganesh-Ganapati's power as travellers' friend and facilitator?

Focussing intently still on the territory of the body, Mr Singh's well-endowed snout is now guiding his long-lashed eyes and fine fingers in the extraction of a splinter from Ms Pierce's bejewelled big toe. An outstanding specimen of a probing proboscis finds wood at last.

Rubbing shoulders and other body parts, East and West converge, oblivious of the magnificent mastodon who, once riled, can charge full pelt against petty cultural games, knocking empires aside at will. These players are not upright, topiary figures, primmed, trimmed and hedged about for social display, nor will they ever be while passion overruns pretension. Rather, they're flexing flesh and feelings in flux, water waxing and waning, breath and bone, air and ether, languidness and luscious light.

My eyes flicker across to the compact icon dangling in front of my taxidriver's windscreen. A wink and a sparkle.

### In adoration: elephas maximus.
### Sri Ganesh Vandana.

# Time Rules Supreme

The days roll by. Who can devote time to understanding their narrative or where they will lead?

**The day before yesterday** was a lesson in mental torture. Or, rather, how not to allow the weighing of time to become a torture to the mind.

I had to submit an application for new office space. Without it I'd have to cart all my office furniture of desks and chairs out onto the street for garbage collection. Of course I'm joking. But what to do with them? As well as a double filing cabinet filled with documents (yes, I'm old school about paper files which have a more substantial place in my existence than computer files which can so easily be passed over as ethereal and forgettable). And paintings hanging on the walls, a large square of Persian carpet, a couple of chests, a fridge and kitchenware, and books, books, books. Once a writer, now I'm a publishing administrator and marketer of books – mine and a stable of authors growing by the month. If I couldn't manage to submit the application for office space that day, my business treasure trove might have to dissipate, my business atrophy, my identity and my planned future of untold wealth become the stuff of dreams forever unfulfilled.

So I sat to attention all day in my confined office with no fresh air or window to the world and wrote about my company's mission and vision … to mentor committed emerging writers and publish their work, with the associated activities of promoting and marketing, including organising public readings of their work and the filming of these events.

My arm was sore. I'd been suffering RSI, having massage treatment and continuing to type and hold my elbow in a crooked position while texting and making phone calls. How could I not? I'm making my mark on the world, a microcosm though it is. My company's mark …

It took quite a few hours to fill in the boxes of responses to specific questions, using effective terminology to cover the appropriate policy issues paramount in the minds of the panel of bureaucrats who would judge the applications. Just like writing a high school or university essay, really, even though the arguments put forward needed to be delivered in 300 or 400 word segments, a pedantic process following a thorough reading of the policy guidelines.

That wasn't the hard part of the process though. What was hard was working while waiting for delivery of a coup de grace, a video which would show the actual public performance by our writers just a few days earlier. I'd had a major difference of opinion about the quality of the video with its producer the day before – he'd refused to make editing changes, walked out of my office with arrogant posture and stride, & then at home relented, saying he'd drop in a revised version, first thing in the morning, later revised to 2 or 3 pm.

When he arrived at 3.30, the file was too large for me to view on my laptop, so he showed me his Apple laptop version. It was only after he'd left that I found I could neither upload the CD (I'd asked for a USB) as part of the online application nor email it to anyone from my laptop. I had to wait for a colleague to arrive at 4.30 to use his computer, so I tried to send him various other files I was unable to upload as well. When he arrived 25 minutes before the 5pm deadline, it was something of a frenzy to sort out what could or couldn't be uploaded, before deciding to simply include the url of our website and have the producer upload the file to our website via Youtube that evening. We made the deadline by one and a half minutes. Breath-holding stuff. Does this sound all a bit technically difficult? I'm a writer, a lover of words, so of course I'm entirely capable and at ease about spending most of each day at my computer sorting out IT conundrums. NOT (at ease) – I meant to say.

Yes, those conundrums were hard … but, as I said, the worst was waiting, staring at the screen for hours, trying again and again to upload files, edited back in case their size was causing the glitches, and photos which I would crop again and again in the same vain hope. And waiting on a support letter from another colleague who had told me he'd have it ready for me to pick up that day, but was strangely absent from phone, email and text communication. And, as I described, waiting for that video which finally arrived mid-afternoon. Again, waiting for a colleague who would deliver salvation. I wasn't brave enough to say, 'Damn! I'm going for a walk in the sun'. And finally saved from my fearful mood, my frustrated tension, by an act of kindness from a new yet close and reliable friend who shares my interests and sense of the rewards of hard work.

**Yesterday** was a fresh start. It could have been torture but I decided I wasn't going to go through that kind of agony again. I went into the office for a couple of hours and told another colleague I was going to do whatever I wanted. I had my arm massaged mid-morning, and planned a long lunch break. I even drove to a ferry wharf to take a ride on the harbour, but just missed the ferry, so I decided that as storm clouds were beginning to gather, it was a much better idea to lounge around near the wharf to catch the last of the interplay of intermittent sun and cloud. I found a park, then a quiet isolated spot sheltered from the wind by a hedge, I dropped my coat onto the lawn, and I lay down and ate half a falafel roll that I'd kept from dinner the night before. Filled with baba ganoush, not hommus. Spicy! The best!

Relaxed, I rang a friend but the line was so bad I couldn't hear her voice very well. She tried to tell me a story several times and I couldn't catch vital words. She persisted, and for her sake I tried to pretend I could hear, to spare her telling it a fourth time, but it was hard to know whether to agree, using a 'mm, mm' or a neutral, 'oh'. To sound surprised, pleased, shocked. I could only be led by her tone of voice … but she saw through, or heard, my deception. So we giggled away the frustration which on that day I was not prepared to even acknowledge, in stark contrast to other days when we might have been plunged into a fever of tension over a bad phone line. I told her the words didn't matter, I was just glad to hear her voice.

'Sing me a song?' I pleaded. 'Would you?' Not such an unusual request made of this contralto known for her repertoire of sacred songs. About 10 seconds of silence kept me wondering whether she was deciding which song, preparing her throat for warbling, still tossing up whether to sing at all, or maintaining a stubborn silence of refusal. Just wait patiently, I told myself. Don't waver. Maintain this expectation of pleasure in your mind. And a gentle rhythmic sound began to travel down the phone line, much clearer than the previous stunted vocabulary we'd struggled to understand. Still I couldn't understand the words, yet I knew the mood – was it sadness? No, more subtle – wistfulness. Later I learnt that the song was a morning prayer, and the final line was a wish for universal love. When our conversation ended, I lay on the grass behind the hedge windbreak, looking across the vast expanse of choppy harbour and up at the great canvas of sky, as its turbulent, billowing clouds gathered momentum. I'm blessed, I told myself. Truly blessed, whenever I stop wrangling with myself to see and hear and feel what plenitude surrounds me.

**Today?** Well, I've come into my office and decided to write a diary, using principally my right hand. To try to catch the tenor of my life these days, in recalling and recounting three consecutive days' activities and moods. Whenever I use my left arm it hurts, so I try to restrict myself to typing with my right arm only. I feel fine. I don't have anyone badgering me about time or demanding attention. The day is still early – I have unrealistic hopes of high achievement and financial breakthroughs in the late afternoon. I can expect friendship, both close and precise and far and wide. Offered by people through thinking, speaking, touching, fetching and carrying for me, and I for them – and, finally through the miracles of post-modern science: phoning, texting and going online. I'm caught in the net of this worldwide information revolution, making and taking the best of it. There's a light drizzle outside but I'm warm in this protective shelter of a wired office, window or no window. Later, I may take a short walk outside and feel the force of nature offering renewal to the world.

**By tomorrow ...** I could find time enough to feel the sun again. I might steal my birthright of freedom to escape this cage of contemporary literature which I have willingly entered. To offer up my gratitude to the universe that has created the passage of my life within this cocoon of spoken and written words, nurture and love.

There are ways to measure the passage of time outside of the daily grind. To take time in hand, and weigh its value. To slow its pace within the moment. To look into a face. To watch the grace of a single movement. To take a first step and feel its grounding power. To smell a perfume, detect an odour. To tune into a beat; to hear a silence. To feel a presence between two minds.

**Finally,** to love the favour time grants us in experiencing now.

# Over Seas

*This trip reminds me of S.I. Ramanujan.*

*Who?*

*S.I. Do you know him?*

*No. Who is he?*

*A great mathematician.*

*Oh. No, perhaps we don't know him so well in the West. Does he still live in India – or has he migrated?*

*No, no, no. Fifty years ago, a hundred, maybe more ... he was a very dear friend of Mr Thomas Hardy. Do you know Thomas Hardy?*

*Yes, I know of him. Of course. Tess is a rare ...*

*Yes, he visited Thomas Hardy in England – and he wrote of this trip afterwards.*

Such is the tenor of the conversations I have from Sydney with Kriya[1], a Bangalore student of 'The Beats', in the lead-up to his first overseas trip for poetry readings and a lecture tour

---

[1] Both a Tamil and Sanskrit name for a man meaning 'literary composition, energy, ability, knowledge or accomplishment'.

in Australia.

Kriya is going through a major transformation, from chrysalis to butterfly or bee. It's a delight to witness, or rather to hear, the changes floating down the phone line. I'm left wondering what the great S.I. thought and wrote about England, what the friendship consisted of, and what Kriya himself thinks of the bewitched and tragic Tess, who sacrificed her all – security, domesticity, honour. All for love. For love alone, as the equally courageous Christina Stead would have said.

And where did Tess end up? On the vast, cruel, windswept Salisbury Plain, where I'd wandered among the massive pillars of Stonehenge on my first trip to England twenty years before, marvelling at their vast size and astronomical accuracy, with Hardy's magnificent fallen woman on my mind. A woman to be admired. But not emulated, surely?

I don't have a chance to contribute these thoughts to the conversation as Kriya is off again on another creative whimsy.

*You know, I'd like to give a friend of mine who's writing an essay – not an essay, more like an extended letter or diary, or even memoir, it's fictional – I'd like to give her one delicate, Dravidian, ancient Sangam poem that I know from the hills of Karnataka, about an exquisite butterfly, injured, that lands on a young man's shoulders and, to assist her, he flies further than he's ever imagined, back to her water country ...*

But wait, I'm thinking .... If only I could get a grip on the first part of this conversation in the midst of the strident traffic noise accompanying Kriya as he explains that he's 'on the road'. I dare not cross-examine him about detail or I'll be distracted from the entrancing pleasure of following the natural flow of his thoughts.

I can recall I have heard of a brilliant Indian mathematician from South India who had a friendship with a Trinity College, Cambridge, mathematician called G.H. Hardy, not the novelist, Thomas. Some story about G.H. Hardy visiting the Indian fellow in hospital in London and complaining about a taxicab registration plate number being boring and therefore a bad omen – whatever that might mean in the language of numbers and the minds of numbers men – and the Indian fellow putting him right, explaining that it wasn't a boring number at all, in fact it was the smallest number for ... something to do with two cubes. Who even knows now what the number was?

These characters – the mathematicians – were around in the early 1900s, as was Thomas Hardy. So Thomas Hardy may even have got into the mathematical mix – there's no way I can refute it. Regardless, Kriya may be forgiven for confusing these two Hardys – novelist and mathematician – from such a distant past and exotic culture as pre-WWI Britain. Now, at least, I won't have to ponder Tess's fate any further, the back of my mind is advising my frontal lobes, as I tune in again to Kriya's buzzing mobile phone commentary.

For Kriya, who's about the same age now as I was when I wandered in the midst of Stonehenge, is just testing his wings in the wide world, after many years of hardship – that is, financial penury and emotional frustration on a scale still common in India and rare in Australia. These days he has purpose and, suddenly, too much to do. When I first met him he told me he was a poet. Good heavens, I thought, that's not a serious endeavour for a young man who wants to make something of himself!

'Take care, womankind,' was my second thought, as I was wary of the emotional mire into which a girlfriend of mine plunged when she fell in love with one of his ken. This fellow needs to be rescued from his own entangling romantic maze, this soft-focus view of himself – or he'll end up fat, forty and financially broke, I figured. Soon I discovered he was fixed on the idea of a literary life, and had received several awards in support of his fixation.

A year later, as we chat on the phone, he has a lot on his mind that needs attending to. He's completing an MPhil on 'Beat' poetry, sitting exams for a teaching certificate, helping to organise an international literary conference, all while applying for a visa for the brief research and lecture visit to Australia. I thought a tourist visa would be easy and quick to obtain, and would suffice for his recreational and research purposes, but I should have realised nothing is quick and easy in India, and a tourist visa impossible to obtain without extensive financial records to prove you have the wherewithal to get yourself back to India for good. As Kriya explains … and I find out when I am called on – along with his father, his academic supervisor and various other authority figures – to provide testimony of the authenticity of Kriya's intellectual intentions in Australia and his financial support in India.

The paperwork is all very trying and long-winded, and Kriya is so stressed he ends up in bed with what he calls a 'compressed disc' – not the 'full slipped disc' he suffered a few years back, he reassures himself. But it's so debilitating that he has to call on his many sympathetic classmates and friends to type his thesis bibliography. Before he reaches that stage of deterioration (which I note lasts just a few days – long enough for the bibliography to be completed) he's quite surprised that he's become so competent, able to switch from administrivia required by the travel agent for submission of his visa application, to the demands of deep thinking in pulling the strands of his thesis on Dravidian poetry together.

*It reminds me of Napoleon.*
*What does?*
*What is happening to my mind.*
*What is happening to it?*
*Napoleon was famous, you know, for being able to move instantly from one*
*thinking task to another. Without a trouble. Smoothly.*
*Oh, yes, I'm sure he had a great mind.*

I'm wanting to talk about Napoleon's 'common man' approach to military generalship, how he would actually lead his troops into battle, on horseback admittedly, but prepared to face the enemy with full courage and thereby instill confidence in his men – in contrast to the weasel-y politicians of today who send young men to their deaths in the far-flung reaches of Iraq or Afghanistan – even Pakistan – on some pretext of national security, with crocodile weeping for the boys' mothers during national media conferences where these spin doctors savour their own self-righteous cant. Yet, still on the question of Napoleon's greatness, I see clearly that despite his valour, he was an aggressive expansionist, put simply, a self-appointed monarch and autocrat, an egomaniac who rampaged and killed in the name of the splendour of the French nation, and finally failed to defeat the even more forceful English imperialists at Waterloo. Even so, he loved Josephine with a single passion and she was not a young woman when he met her. He was struck by her 'spirit, sweetness and beauty' as well as her older woman's 'mystique'.

*The bare root of the bean is pink*
*like the leg of a jungle hen,*
*and herds of deer attack its overripe pods.*
*For the harshness*
*of this season of morning dew*
*there is no cure*
*but the breast of my man[2].*

[2] Allur Nanmullai Kuruntokai 68', A.K. Ramanujan (tr) Poems of Love and War (Delhi: Oxford University Press, 1985) 21.

But I don't have a chance to offer Kriya any ideas of links between concepts of universal love, and legends about commoners and kings that cross cultural boundaries, for he's off and away on his own Napoleonic fancies.

*You see, I can perfectly leave the visa business and go into my writing without a trouble. Then I'm called back to the documents, and the phone calls, and the bother I'm causing my father who has to give up his financial details. Do you think it will be okay if the date on the bank statement is not able to be read – you see it is smudged – will it be acceptable, do you think, after all? As I am saying, I will leave all these matters, and perfectly return to my thoughts, to carry on till the end of the chapter. It's a surprise to me. I can create categories and move from one box to another.*

And I recall Kriya's last summer lounging about at his home in hill country in the south, once his Uni course had ended. His voice resonated, deep and heavy from sleeping in, the intense tropical heat taking over his body and mind, his soporific stupor punctuated by a fan's regular clicking through the heavy background soundscape of blaring traffic and crows cawing, the inevitable crows of India seeping into the texture of my life in Australia.

*What will I do, he would ask me? This is my last chance to get 'on the track'. I must take it – and help my father. I don't want to be a burden. But what must I do next'*
*The answer lies with God,* I'd tell him over and over.

Kriya's thoughts would veer between the frantic and the dulled. Any effort to haul himself out of his familial village life seemed overwhelming. Today he exhibits a completely different, invigorated mindset and I respond in kind.

*Yes, the mind is remarkable, isn't it? So versatile and powerful. The Buddhists picture a classification system in their minds as an aid to memory, imagining the mind as a great library, so they can mentally walk down aisle after aisle, turning into row after row, reaching into box after box for folder after folder to catalogue a piece of information or retrieve it.*

*Which Buddhists are they?*

*Tibetan Buddhists.*
*Oh, I see. I can do the same.*

To be able to swap ideas about the nature and capacity of one's mind with someone is a wondrous thing. To attempt to keep track of one's thinking. To watch its working. These are the conversations we share.

And then there are the reflections about Kriya's love of 'thinai' poetry, and his recitation:

*What She Said*

*Bigger than earth, certainly,*
*higher than the sky,*
*more unfathomable than the waters*
*is this love for this man*
*of the mountain slopes*
*where bees make rich honey*
*from the flowers of the kurinci*
*that has such black stalks[3].*

Then Kriya's projections about what lies ahead in his life follow:

*I've been thinking about what Australia will be like. I'm a little bit frightened,*
*you see. I won't know anyone else – except for you. Oh, yes, there is someone*
*– he's the son of the First Minister of our state. What do you think, shall I*
*meet him?*
*Of course, you must meet him. But where does he live? Is he in Sydney or*
*another city?*
*I don't know. I'm not sure. I have not the details yet.*
*Well, I hope he's in Sydney because it would be costly to visit him in another*
*city. Try to find out soon, eh?*

---

[3]Tevakulattar Kuruntokai 3', Ramanujan 5.

*I will. And another concern – there will be none of my friends. You will be working.*

*No, I'll organise the talks for you, and work with some of my coaching clients, but I'll still have a lot of time to be with you. And you'll meet new people. You can wander off to explore on your own, too. You're used to being on your own, you know. You live alone in the hostel ...*

*Not that way. It's another thing.*

*Is it the distance? It's not much further than Delhi, really, and you were fine there on your own.*

*It's leaving the land. Travelling over seas. I had a dream that all the passengers were preparing to crash into the sea... all was calm ... but then I think that it was just my imagination, thinking fearful thoughts before I went to sleep. Not a real dream.*

(Whatever that is, a 'real' dream, I wonder.)

*It will be great, Kriya, just great. You'll love it. And isn't it such a lucky thing that you've chosen Australia, that you're coming to a country where the people are so friendly? Besides, where's your sense of adventure? You know, a sunburnt country, a land of sweeping plains[4] ...*

No plantation or hill country. No field or coppice. I think of Tess, for some reason.

*As I walked over Salisbury Plain*
*Oh, there I met this scamping young blade.*
*He kissed me and enticèd me so[5] ...*

Then, once the visa is lodged, a new phase. Not a word, not a comment about the journey now imminent. Kriya seems to be positively cosmopolitan. It's all the same to him: here, there, anywhere. He has his first ever job, you see, and it's consuming his full attention.

---

[4] Dorothea Mackellar's poem 'Core of My Heart' (later 'A Sunburnt Country') was written while she was living as an expatriate in London in 1908.

[5] 'Salisbury Plain' collected in 1904 by Ralph Vaughan Williams for The Penguin Book of English Folk Songs.

Coming completely out of the wide blue yonder. Paid employment – to start immediately. He had explained that he first had to go to Australia, but he's been told he must begin work straight away, and then take leave, if permitted, for the ten-day trip. He's been appointed a research assistant to a professor at the prestigious IIT – the Institute of Indian Technology – in Bangalore where all those greatly-admired engineers and IT specialists exported to multinational companies in London, New York and California hail from.

*So is the professor impressed that you're coming to Australia?*
*I suppose. But that's not why he chose me.*
*Why did he choose you?*
*He saw me at the hospital.*

(Is this about his back, I wonder?)

*Were you in hospital, Kriya?*
*Not I. My friend.*
*Which friend?*
*Dinesh. I went to visit him there. And I was talking to his professor.*
*So it was like a job interview in the hospital ward?*
*He was impressed by two things. One was that I was a good friend, that I had visited Dinesh when he needed me. The second thing was that I was doing my MPhil. I didn't say that I was a poet. I don't think that people are impressed by it.*

(No kidding!)

*Poets aren't usually too reliable, eh?*
*No.* (He laughs.)

I'm not the only one looking out for Kriya's material future, it seems. I've noticed that he attracts Good Samaritans wherever he goes. People feel they need to protect him from his gentle compassionate nature, I'm sure. Bolster him. Tend to his needs. Just like all those girls in Cochin who flutter about, offering to translate his poetry at the blink of an eye.

*But surely he snapped you up once he heard that you would be coming on a lecture tour to Australia?*

*No, it is as I say.*

*What hours do you work?*

*Oh, the professor decides my hours. I come when he says, and I leave when he says.*

*Oh, that sounds perfect. Are you a slave then?*

*Yes, that is right. But at the end of the month will come the pay.*

*Yes, there's a name for that. Do you know what it is?*

*No.*

*You're a wage slave.*

*Yes, a wage slave. But every job has the same, isn't it? The same conditions, or similar. You must do what the boss says.*

*But what about your trip? Are you thinking about it? Are you happy, excited, about coming?*

*Cherie, you must know that these days we have a very good idea about other countries, from internet and television, and so forth.*

He hasn't got a clue, but how can I tell him so without seeming to belittle him. To live the experience of a foreign culture is on another scale completely from watching a documentary.

*Okay. But are you happy about it still?*

(He's snickering.)

*Why do you laugh? What is it?*

*I'm wondering how many times you will ask me that question. Do Australians really care so much about whether I am happy to see their country?*

Sharp-witted and usually gentle is Kriya. He's very adept in the realm of the emotions, mostly projecting sensitivity, careful not to cause offence. A mother's boy, he's admiring of a senior feminist lecturer in Cochin, is always keen to improve his English through constructive criticism, and to learn about other cultures. Suddenly there seems to be a strengthening of his volition and his backbone. Maybe it's the professor's influence and the research subject Kriya has been given: Masculine Studies. A coming of age.

*What She Said*

*to her girl friend*
*On the tall hill*
*where the short-stemmed nightshade quivers,*
*a squatting cripple*
*sights a honey hive*
*above,*
*points to the honey,*
*cups his hands,*
*and licks his fingers;*
*so too,*
*even if one's lover*
*doesn't love or care,*
*it still feels good*
*inside*
*just to see him*
*now and then*[6].

\*

So I'm held in suspense – waiting, wondering. Will Kriya's deceptively delicate butterfly wings provide enough resilience to negotiate the fierce southerlies of the Indian Ocean, allowing him to show off so many glittering hues in Sydney? Is his bee sting potent enough to close the watery gap between a 'sub' continent and the 'great south land'?

I'll find out soon enough – once he dons the woolly 'sweaters' needed for wintry August in Australia. No perspiration required.

At least he won't have to face snow, as did S.I. Ramanujan, who at first resisted the idea of voyaging from his home in South India to England for further study, due to religious restrictions on travelling abroad. Yet once transported, S.I. remained a deeply religious mathematician, praising the hillside goddess Namagiri, for his talent, and declaring to the world beyond his cloistered culture that, 'an equation for me has no meaning unless it expresses a

---

[6]'Paranar Kurutokai 60', Ramanujan 15.

thought of God.' S.I.'s theorems are now used extensively in computer science, a basis for the information explosion overtaking the entire globe.

'Her arms across her breast she laid; She was more fair than words can say,' Kriya recites to me along a fibre optic phone line before he packs his mobile away. At last, a beggar girl makes good as a king lifts her up out of poverty. 'This beggar maid shall be my queen!' Tennyson declared in a universal aesthetic of hope for the salvation of the pure and beautiful ones through love alone[7].

Recognition of the poem across ages and cultures, space and time, hints that in sharing a common language, we commonly share a colonial literary mind, the product of English culture predating even the Hardys' day, snippets of which we've archived in our respective thought-vaults. All filed in separate catalogues and dispersed among disparate societies as part of the one mind that is God, some forms labelled 'exotic', some called 'home page'.

Now fully prepped, carrying a head full of poetry and a backpack slung over his shoulder, Kriya reinforces his protective sting for travelling as his hard sheath of chrysalis falls away, thrusting him forward to take flight.

*

The saga climaxes beside Sydney's great well of a gleaming harbour, as Kriya uses his natural tongue to speak a universal language, gifting me a divine offering, pure poetry flowing directly from his ancestors.

*What She Said*

*Like moss on water*
*in the town's water tank,*
*this body's pallor*
*clears*
*as my lover touches*
*and touches*

---

[7]'The Beggar Maid' by Alfred Lord Tennyson published in 1842, shortly after the Napoleonic era.

*and spreads again,*
*as he lets go,*
*as he lets go*[8].

[8] 'Paranar Kuruntokai 399', Ramanujan 30.

# No Title

*To imagine ... in your mind only colours and shapes of trees, rivers, the sky, the earth.*

*No word games. Tricks of tongue. Simply pictures of the natural world – the only world. A mindscape brimming with light and movement.*

*No urban disturbances. No concrete. No brick walls. No degrees of grey suit, black suit, blue suit, and the shades of meaning in the colour of collars and ties. No plastic toys – for any age group, child or adult.*

*No hard cold tiles or timber boards underneath flat leather shoe, underneath sock, underneath sole of foot. Imagine only the strength and mass of stone felt directly beneath your foot's skin. Lying down on your belly to hug the warmth of a great slab of rock which has soaked up the afternoon sun and radiates the heat into your flesh and, deeper still, your bones.*

*Consciousness accepts the images around you without distance: sparkle of light skimming the surface of a river; shimmer of shapes in windy leaves; broad tree trunks that arch in slow movement; a goanna rustling dry tinder; a platypus stirring the mud of a clear billabong; an echidna nosing the powder dust of dry soil; a kookaburra watches; cockatoos flap and screech. Flickers in sight and sound – no difference between seeing and seen, hearing and heard. Only thoughts of action within the balance of place.*

*A hungry belly brings attention to food: that is the time that an animal is sighted. Believing that prey appear for the purpose of being taken as nourishment underlies a bond established in ritual. There's no chase, simply a dance played out between hunter and food source, forager and earth provision. The act of killing the quarry or plucking the fruit as important as the ceremonial act which brings the food into being. Singing and dancing a love of the earth shares meaning with eating its produce. All activities are carried out in a harmony which is the natural surround. As without, so within.*

*The images of the mind are the perceptions of the senses. Pictures seen through the eyes form images in the mind. The touch in a hand forms a ripple of thought. Hearing piques attention. The nose tweaks a memory. The comfort in common of mouth and belly. No transposition. To know in the round, from above, below, beside, from the interior of earth and space as one.*

*The fingers of the hand just one part of a whole sensual body, as toes, chest, lips, forehead all reach out for impression. Sight, touch, smell, hearing, taste – all agents of subtle extra-sensory power.*

*Dreams guide the wanderer. Messages tell what must be done and what avoided. Those beings who appear are meant to appear. There are no hypotheticals, no missed opportunities, no greener pastures. All is of the land enduring; no ambitions to fulfil. The cycle of the days is the cycle of the ages of birth, death, rebirth. Ancestors are present. The future exists now. No rush to arrive or depart.*

*Red earth, brown soil, black mud, silver quartz rock, buff sandstone, cream-coloured sand. Climbing, running, leaping. Scouring for plants, painting story, cutting skin to let the red sap spurt.*

*As the matriarch shapes out of bloody labour, the youth grows scars for lore.*

*From earth to earth, belonging.*

C V Williams is an Australian writer with a long-held interest in Indian culture. She has moved into the short fiction genre after publication of several biographies of international and national figures. So far she's enjoying the freedom that writing fiction allows an author to play with words to create light and shade, sadness and joy.

# Picture Sources

Whose nose was this? Trust, Balmy Bali, Mother Earth – Father Land, Pearly Shells: C V Williams

A Footnote on Footlights, Smoke Dream: Ferdinando Manzo

Black Magic, Anticipation, A Green Thumb and a Lotus Hand: C V Williams & Wikipedia

Baisant des Fleurs, The Solace of Daughters, a glistening afternoon, Sydney Syd: C V Williams

A Nonconformist Spirit Guide: Wikipedia

Turning Fifty: C V Williams

Travelling with Ganesh: C V Williams & pexels

Time Rules Supreme: C V Williams

Over Seas: pexels

No title: C V Williams

Author Background: Deepa N